SO-AEF-567

The Slater Sisters of Montana

Nestled in the Rocky Mountains,
the idyllic Lazy S Ranch is about to welcome home
the beautiful Slater sisters.

Don your Stetson and your cowboy boots and join
us as these sisters experience first loves,
second chances and their very own happy-ever-
afters with the most delicious heroes in the West.
No dream is too big in Montana!

Out first in August 2013

THE COWBOY SHE COULDN'T FORGET

followed in November 2013 by

PROPOSAL AT THE LAZY S RANCH

Dear Reader,

This is the second book in my Slater Sisters series.
Josie is the second-oldest daughter and a twin.
Reluctantly she comes back home to Montana to help
her estranged father, Colt Slater, after his stroke, and
to help with the survival of the family ranch. What she
doesn't expect is to be reunited with her high school
sweetheart, Garrett Temple.

Garrett broke her heart nearly ten years ago. Worse,
after they went their separate ways, he married another
woman. A woman he'd gotten pregnant.

Now her ex is the building contractor working on the
family business venture. Josie has to be with him every
day to get the guest lodge finished in time for her sister
Ana's wedding.

Garrett has never gotten over Josie, but now is not the
time to think about rekindling anything, because he has
a son to raise. Brody has to come first in his life.

So over the next month, not only does she have to deal
with rebuilding a relationship with her father, she has to
work daily with the man she couldn't forget.

I hope you enjoy this second book as much as I
enjoyed writing it.

Patricia Thayer

Proposal at the Lazy S Ranch

Patricia Thayer

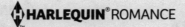

HARLEQUIN® ROMANCE

If you purchased this book without a cover you should be aware that this book is stolen property. It was reported as "unsold and destroyed" to the publisher, and neither the author nor the publisher has received any payment for this "stripped book."

Recycling programs
for this product may
not exist in your area.

ISBN-13: 978-0-373-74264-6

PROPOSAL AT THE LAZY S RANCH

First North American Publication 2013

Copyright © 2013 by Patricia Wright

All rights reserved. Except for use in any review, the reproduction or utilization of this work in whole or in part in any form by any electronic, mechanical or other means, now known or hereafter invented, including xerography, photocopying and recording, or in any information storage or retrieval system, is forbidden without the written permission of the publisher, Harlequin Enterprises Limited, 225 Duncan Mill Road, Don Mills, Ontario M3B 3K9, Canada.

This is a work of fiction. Names, characters, places and incidents are either the product of the author's imagination or are used fictitiously, and any resemblance to actual persons, living or dead, business establishments, events or locales is entirely coincidental.

This edition published by arrangement with Harlequin Books S.A.

For questions and comments about the quality of this book, please contact us at CustomerService@Harlequin.com.

® and TM are trademarks of Harlequin Enterprises Limited or its corporate affiliates. Trademarks indicated with ® are registered in the United States Patent and Trademark Office, the Canadian Trade Marks Office and in other countries.

Printed in U.S.A.

www.Harlequin.com

Originally born and raised in Muncie, Indiana, **Patricia Thayer** is the second of eight children. She attended Ball State University, and soon afterward headed west. Over the years she's made frequent visits back to the Midwest, trying to keep up with her growing family.

Patricia has called Orange County, California, home for many years. She enjoys not only the warm climate, but also the company and support of other published authors in the local writers' organization. For the past eighteen years she has had the unwavering support and encouragement of her critique group. It's a sisterhood like no other.

When she's not working on a story, you might find her traveling the United States and Europe, taking in the scenery and doing story research while thoroughly enjoying herself, accompanied by Steve, her husband for over thirty-five years. Together they have three grown sons and four grandsons. As she calls them: her own true-life heroes. On rare days off from writing you might catch her at Disneyland, spoiling those grandkids rotten! She also volunteers for the Grandparent Autism Network.

Patricia has written for over twenty years, and has authored more than forty-six books. She has been nominated for both a National Readers' Choice Award and the prestigious RITA® Award. Her book *Nothing Short of a Miracle* won an RT Reviewers' Choice Award.

A longtime member of Romance Writers of America, she has served as president and held many other board positions for her local chapter in Orange County. She's a firm believer in giving back.

Check her website, www.patriciathayer.com, for upcoming books.

Recent books by Patricia Thayer

THE COWBOY SHE COULDN'T FORGET*
HER ROCKY MOUNTAIN PROTECTOR****
SINGLE DAD'S HOLIDAY WEDDING****
THE COWBOY COMES HOME**
ONCE A COWBOY...***
TALL, DARK, TEXAS RANGER***
THE LONESOME RANCHER***
LITTLE COWGIRL NEEDS A MOM***

*Slater Sisters of Montana
**The Larkville Legacy
***The Quilt Shop in Kerry Springs
****Rocky Mountain Brides

Other titles by this author available in ebook format at www.Harlequin.com.

To Timothy Paul Brooks, Jr.
You were too young to leave us,
but you'll never be forgotten.
RIP Timmy. March 19, 1990–February 26, 2013.

CHAPTER ONE

SHE WAS A COWARD.

Josefina Slater jumped into her BMW and drove away from the Lazy S Ranch, her childhood home. Before she'd left California two days ago for Montana, she'd told herself she would be able to come back here and help with her father's recovery from a stroke. But when she'd arrived at the house and saw her older sister, Ana, she found she wasn't ready to face Colton Slater, or her past.

When Josie had arrived at the ranch house and was greeted by her older sister, Ana, she froze right there on the spot. She needed more time. She told her sister she wasn't ready and got back into her car and started driving. To where, she had no idea.

She'd grown up here on the ranch with a man who didn't want the daughters Lucia Slater left behind when she walked out. Outside of her siblings, her twin, Tori, and older sister, Ana, and younger sister, Marissa, there hadn't been much else to keep her here. This was Josie's first time back in nearly ten years.

About two miles down the road, she opened the window. The air was brisk, reminding her that winter was fast approaching. With the quiet hum of the engine mingled with soft music from the radio, she finally started to relax.

She glanced out the windshield at the rolling green pastures that seemed to go on for miles and was framed by the scenic Rocky Mountains. Tall pines covered the slopes as the majestic peaks reached upward to the incredible blue sky.

Quite a different landscape from her home in Los Angeles, or her life. Success in her career as an event planner came with a lot of hard work and little sleep. Except she'd been told if she didn't stop her hectic pace, her health could be in serious trouble. To help ease her stress, her doctor suggested she take time off. Tori, her twin sister and partner in Slater Style, had been the one who'd insisted she come back here to the ranch and try to relax.

Sure, returning here was going to ease her stress. Right. She couldn't even get through the front door.

Her grip tightened on the steering wheel. No. she wouldn't let Colt Slater turn her back into that insecure little girl. She shook her head. "Not again." She wouldn't let any man do that to her.

She continued to drive down the road until she could see part of the Big Hole River. Memories flooded her head, reminding her how she and her sisters used to sneak off and swim there. That brought a smile to her lips. It was also where Ana was building the new lodge along with some small fishing cabins. They'd hoped to add income to help the other problem, the Lazy S's struggling finances.

Curiosity had Josie turning off onto a dirt road and driving the half mile to where several trucks were parked. She pulled in next to a crew cab pickup that had GT Construction embossed on the side.

Why not check out the progress? Anything to delay her going back to the house. She climbed out, glad she'd worn her jeans and boots, and pulled her lined jacket closer to her body, shielding her from the late-October weather.

Feeling excitement for the project she'd helped create with Ana, she headed across the grass toward the river to observe the progress of the two-story log cabin structure taking shape about thirty yards from the water's edge.

"Good job, Ana," she breathed into the cool autumn breeze.

Suddenly someone called out, but before she

could turn around she felt something hit her in the back, sending her flying. Josie let out a cry as she hit the hard ground.

Garrett Temple felt pain shoot through his body as he cradled the small woman under him. It took a few breaths to get his lungs working from the impact, but at least he'd kept her from getting hit by the lumber truck. He managed to roll off her as his men started to gather around.

"I didn't see her, boss," Jerry said as he leaned over them. "You okay?"

Garrett nodded, but his attention was on the still woman facedown on the grass. He knelt beside the petite body and traced over her for any broken bones or visible injuries.

"You want me to call the paramedics?" someone asked.

"Give me a minute," Garrett said as he gently brushed back the long whiskey-colored hair from her face. He froze as recognition hit him. The olive skin, the delicate jawline, long dark lashes. He knew that underneath those closed lids were mesmerizing blue eyes. His heart began to pound even more rapidly. "Josie?"

She groaned, and he said her name again. "Josie. Can you hear me?"

With another groan, she started to raise her head. He stopped her, but caught a whiff of her familiar scent. Hell, how could he remember what she smelled like? He drew back, already feeling the familiar pull to this woman. It had been nearly ten years.

She rolled to one side.

"Take it easy," he told her. "Do you hurt anywhere?"

"My chest," she whispered. "Hard to breathe."

"You got the wind knocked out of you."

She blinked and finally opened her eyes, and he was hit with her rich blue gaze. She looked confused, and then said, "Garrett?"

He rose to his knees. "Hello, Josie."

Josie felt as if she were in a dream. Garrett Temple? It couldn't be… She blinked again, suddenly realizing it was reality. She pushed him away, sat up and groaned at the pounding in her head. "What are you doing here?"

He didn't look any happier to see her. "Trying to save your neck."

"Like I need your help for anything." She glanced up and saw several men peering at them. "I'm fine." She brushed off her sweater and jeans, trying to act as if nothing was wrong. "I just need a minute."

The crew didn't move away until Garrett stepped in. "Everyone, this is Ana Slater's sister Josie."

The guys mumbled a quick greeting, and then headed back to their jobs.

Once alone, Josie turned to the man she'd never expected to see again. The man who'd smashed all her dreams and the last person she needed to see right now.

"Do you hurt anywhere?" he asked again.

A broken heart. "No, I'm fine," she lied. Her ankle was suddenly killing her.

Garrett got to his feet and reached down to offer her some help. She got up under her own power, trying to ignore her light-headedness and her throbbing ankle.

"Still as stubborn as ever, I see."

She glared at the large man. He was well over six feet. Nothing had changed in the looks department, either. He was still handsome with all that black wavy hair, not a bald spot in view. Her attention went to his mouth to see that sexy grin, and her stomach tightened in awareness. Well, dang it. She wasn't going to let him get to her again.

She tested some weight on her tender ankle. Not good. "I know why I'm here," she began, "but…why are you?"

He folded his muscular arms over his wide chest. So he'd filled out from the thin boy she once knew in high school.

"I own GT Construction. Ana hired me."

No. Her sister wouldn't do that. Not when she knew how much Garrett had hurt and humiliated her. "We'll see about that." She started to walk off but her ankle couldn't hold her weight and she started to fall.

"Whoa." He caught her in his arms. Big strong arms. "You are hurt."

"No, I just twisted my ankle. I'll be fine when I get back to the ranch."

"You aren't going anywhere until I get you checked out."

"You're not doing anything—" She gasped as he swung her up into his arms as if she were a child. "Put me down," she demanded, but he only drew her closer and she had no choice but to slip her arm around his neck to keep her balance.

He carried her the short distance to his truck. One of the men rushed over and opened the passenger door. Garrett set her down in the seat.

"You can't kidnap me, Garrett." He was so close to her, she could inhale that so-familiar scent of the man she'd once loved more than anything. "Just take me home."

He shook his head. "You were hurt on my construction site, so I'm responsible for you. We're going to the E.R. first, then I'll take you back to the ranch."

She started to speak, but the door got shut in her face. A few minutes later, he appeared in the driver's seat. He handed her purse to her. "You might want to call your sister and tell her where you're going."

"No. She'll get all worried and she has enough on her mind." She stole a glance at the man beside her, unable to stop studying his profile. Okay, so she was curious about him, darn it. "What about my car?"

"I'll have one of the men drive it back to the house."

She folded her arms over her chest.

Garrett started the engine and began to back up, then headed for the highway. "Josie...maybe this would be a good chance to talk."

She glared at him. "What could we possibly have to say to each other, Garrett? I got the message nine years ago when you said, 'Sorry Josie, I'm going to marry someone else.'" She hated that his words still hurt. "So don't waste any more words."

Josie managed to fight back tears. She had to concentrate on getting through this time with a man who broke her heart once. She wasn't going to let it happen again, so she decided to head back to Los Angeles as soon as possible.

An hour later at the emergency room in Dillon, Garrett sat with Josie while they waited for the doctor. Even in the silly gown they had her put on, she still looked good. There was no denying that seeing her again had affected him, more than he thought possible.

From the moment when he noticed Josie Slater in Royerton High School and saw her big blue eyes, he'd been a goner. They'd been a couple all through school, even after he graduated and went off to college. Josie finished high school and went to college locally two years later. Then one weekend he'd come home to tell her about his apprenticeship. They had a big fight about him being gone all summer, and they broke up. Josie refused to talk to him for months. Then he met Natalie....

Now all these years later, Josie was back here. Seeing her today had been harder than he could imagine. But her reaction toward him was a little hard to take. He didn't have to worry about her having any leftover feelings for him.

Garrett stood outside of the cubicle and the curtain was drawn as the doctor examined Josie.

"So, Ms. Slater," the doctor began, "you're getting a nasty bruise on your forehead." There was silence for a moment, and the middle-aged man continued, "You're lucky. It doesn't seem you have a concussion."

Grateful, Garrett sagged against the wall, knowing he shouldn't eavesdrop, but he still listened for more information.

"I want you to take it easy today," the doctor told her. "Your ankle is swollen, but the X-ray didn't show any broken bones. But you'll need to put ice on it." He paused. "Do you take any medications?"

Garrett heard Josie rattle off a few. He recognized one was for anxiety and the other for sleeping. What was wrong with her?

The doctor came out from behind the curtain. "She'll be fine, although she'll have some bruises."

"Thank you, Doctor."

He nodded. "Just make sure she rests today and have her stay off her feet."

"I will."

The doctor walked away, and Garrett called, "You decent?"

"Yes," she grumbled.

He went behind the curtain and found her sitting on the bed, not looking happy. "I got a clean bill of health, so can we go home?"

He nodded, suddenly wishing she was home. But he had a feeling that Josie was headed back to California real soon, and he'd lose her for the second time.

It was another forty minutes before Garrett pulled up in front of the Slater home. Josie's pulse started racing once again as she looked up at the big two-story brown house with the white trim. It was a little faded and the porch needed some work. So a lot of things around the ranch hadn't been cared for in a while.

Garrett got out of the truck and walked around to her side. He pulled the crutches out of the back, but propped them against the side of the truck as he reached in and scooped her into his arms. Instead of setting her down on the ground, he carried her toward the house.

"Hey, I can do this myself."

"It's crazy to struggle with these steps when I can get you in the house faster."

She wasn't going to waste the effort to argue. Soon she'd be inside and he'd be gone.

Garrett paused at the heavy oak door with the cut-glass oval window. She drew a quiet breath and released it. It was bad enough that the man she'd once loved was carrying her around in his arms, but she still had to face the other man in her life. Her father.

"You okay?" Garrett asked.

"Yeah, I'm just peachy."

He stared at her, but didn't say a word. Wise man. He managed to turn the knob and open the door.

Inside, she glanced around. This had been part of the house she hadn't seen much as a child. Everyone used the back door off the kitchen. This was the formal part of the house.

Nothing much had changed over the years, she noted, as Garrett carried her across glossy honey-colored hardwood floors and past the sweeping staircase that led upstairs. He continued down the hall where the living room was closed off by large oak pocket doors. She tensed. Her father's new living quarters since coming home from the hospital.

They finally reached Colt's office. "She's home," Garrett announced as he carried her inside.

Ana Slater glanced up from the computer screen and froze. Her older sister was tall and slender with nearly black hair and blue eyes.

"Josie! Oh, God, what happened?"

"I had a little collision at the construction site."

Garrett set her down in the high-back chair across from the desk. "She'd gotten in the path of a truckload of lumber," he told her. "I pushed her out of the way. She landed funny."

"You mean, *you* landed on me."

Ana glanced back and forth between the two. "When you called me, you said nothing about being injured." She looked concerned. "But you're all right?"

"Yes!"

"No!" Garrett said. "The doctor wants her to rest."

"I need to stay off my ankle, but I have crutches to help get around."

"I'll go get them," Garrett said, and walked out of the room.

Josie turned to her big sister. "So when were you going to tell me that Garrett Temple was building the lodge? Or was it going to remain a secret?"

Ana tried to look innocent and failed. "Okay, how was I supposed to tell you?"

"By telling me the truth."

Josie glanced around the dark paneled room that had been Colt's sanctuary. They'd never been allowed in here, but that didn't seem to bother Ana these days. By the looks of it she'd taken over.

"I'm sorry, Josie. I thought since you said you weren't coming home, I didn't need to say anything."

Josie had trouble hiding her anger. "There have to be other contractors here in town you could have used."

"First of all, Garrett gave us the lowest bid, and some of our own ranch hands are working on the crew. Secondly, he's moved back here and now lives at the Temple Ranch to help out his father."

Josie closed her eyes. It was enough having to deal with her father but now, Garrett. "Then I'm going back to L.A."

"Josie, please. I need you to stay, at least for a little while. We can make it so that you and Garrett don't have any contact." She hesitated, then said, "And Colt, he definitely wants you here. He was so happy when I told him you came home."

Her father wanted her here? That didn't sound like the cold, distant man who'd raised her.

"We all need you here, sis." Ana continued her pitch. "I can't tell you how wonderful it is to have you here, even if it's only for a short time. So please, give it a few days. At least until your ankle is better."

The Lazy S had been her home, once. If Colt had changed like Ana said, she wanted to try and have some sort of relationship with the man. Was it crazy to hope? At the very least, she wanted to help Ana with the financial problems. It was no secret they needed outside income to survive.

Ana and her fiancé, Vance Rivers, the ranch foreman, had already opened the property on their section of the river to anglers. It brought in a nice profit. That was why they were expanding on the business.

Her sister spoke up. "The lodge was your idea to help with income for the ranch. Don't you want to stick around to see your vision come true?"

It had been Josie's idea to build housing to rent out. As an event planner she knew the large structure could be used for company retreats, family reunions and even small weddings. It was to bring in more revenue to help during lean years.

Maybe a little while here wouldn't be so bad. "How soon is this wedding of yours?"

"As soon as possible," came the answer from the doorway.

They both turned and saw Vance Rivers smiling at his future bride.

Ana's grin was just as goofy. "Oh, honey, I don't think I can pull it off that soon."

The sandy-haired man walked across the room dressed in his cowboy garb, including leather chaps. "I'm glad you're home, Josie," he told her. "Ana has missed her sisters."

Josie fought a smile and lost. "Seems to me my big sis has been too busy to miss anyone."

Ana came around the desk and slipped into Vance's arms. Josie couldn't miss the intimate look exchanged between the two. "Yeah, she's miserable all right."

That brought a smile from the handsome man. "A few weeks ago, she was ready to string me up and hang me out to dry."

Josie frowned as she looked at her older sister. "A misunderstanding," Ana said. "It was all resolved and we're all working hard to help the Lazy S and Dad."

"So that was why you hired Garrett?"

"At first I offered to be their partner."

Josie swung around to see Garrett standing in the doorway with her crutches. She stiffened, hating that he still got to her.

Josie didn't want to hear any more from Garrett Temple. "I don't think that will be necessary."

He walked into the room, and Ana and Vance walked out, leaving her alone with the man she once loved more than anything, until he betrayed her. Now, she didn't want to be around him.

With her bum ankle, she was stuck here. That didn't mean she would fall all over this man again.

"I was trying to help out a friend," Garrett said. "And I believe it's a good investment. A lot of ranches have to go into other business to help stay afloat."

"I might be stuck working with you, Temple, but I'm not the same girl who was falling all over you. I've grown up."

"Come on, Josie. What happened between us was years ago."

Eight years and eleven months, she silently

corrected. She could still recall that awful day. She'd been so eager to see him when he returned home. It had been months since their argument. She'd finally agreed to see him, then he broke the devastating news.

He stared at her with those gray eyes, and she still felt the old pull. "I was hoping enough time has passed so…"

"So I'd do what? Forgive you? Forgive you for telling me you loved me, then going off and getting another woman pregnant?"

Later that afternoon in the parlor converted into a first-floor bedroom, Colt Slater sat in his chair in front of the picture window. He squeezed the rubber ball in his right hand. He knew his strength was coming back since the stroke. Just not fast enough to suit him. His therapist, Jay McNeal, kept telling him to have patience. He would get his strength back.

Right now, Colt's concern was for his daughter, Josie. He had watched her drive away from the house and prayed that she would come back, but he wouldn't have bet on it. Not that he could blame her; he hadn't been the best father in the world.

Then a truck pulled up about an hour ago. He held his breath and watched Garrett Temple get out, then lift Josie out of the passenger seat and carry her into the house. He heard the footsteps that went right past his room.

He tensed. What had happened? Had she been in an accident? Finally, Ana came in and explained about Josie's mishap at the construction site with Temple. He wasn't sure he was happy that those two were together again. That man had hurt Josie so badly. He'd wished he could have been there for her back then.

"Will you stop worrying? You're going to end up back in the hospital."

Colt glanced at his friend, Wade Dickson in the chair next to his. Dressed in his usual business suit with his gray hair cut and styled, his friend and lawyer knew all the family secrets.

"I can't stop worrying about Josie," Colt admitted.

"Hey, things worked out with Ana, so there's hope with Josie, too." Wade stood up. "I'll go see what's going on, then I need to get back to my office. Some of us have to work."

Colt nodded. "Thanks for everything, Wade."

"I love those girls, too. It's about time you realize what you have." He turned and walked out.

Alone again, Colt started having doubts again. Would Josie finally come to see him now?

He stood, grabbed the walker and made his way to the sideboard in the dining room. Now it was his exercise area, since he'd been released from the rehab center. He pulled open the drawer and dug under the stack of tablecloths until he found the old album.

Setting it on top, he turned the pages, trying to ignore the ones of his wife, Lucia. He should have burned those years ago, but something kept him from erasing all the past.

He made it to the picture of his four daughters together. The last one taken before their mother walked out the door. His hand moved over the photo. Josie was the one who was a miniature version of her mother, petite and curvy, although her hair was lighter and her eyes were definitely Slater blue.

He frowned, knowing he'd been unfair to his girls. He couldn't even use the excuse of being a single parent. Kathleen, the longtime housekeeper, handled most everything while he worked the ranch. He sighed, recalling those years. Since the day Lucia left, he'd closed up and couldn't show love to his four daughters.

He studied the photo. Analeigh was the oldest. Then came the twins, Josefina Isabel, followed five minutes later by Vittoria Irene. The memory of him standing next to his wife, and encouraging her as she gave birth to their beautiful daughters, Ana, Josie, Tori and Marissa.

He felt tears gathering in his eyes. Would he get the chance to fix the damage he'd done?

"Hello, Colt."

He turned and saw his beautiful Josie leaning against a crutch in the doorway. He'd just been given a second chance, and he wasn't about to throw it away.

CHAPTER TWO

JOSIE FELT STRANGE, not only being back in this house, but seeing her father after all these years.

"J…Josie. I'm gl…glad you're home."

Colt still stood straight and tall as he had before his stroke. Thirty years ago, he'd been a rodeo star, winning the World Saddle Bronc title before he retired when he married Lucia Delgado and brought her back to the Lazy S to make a life, raising cattle and a family.

Now in his mid-fifties, he was still a good-looking man, even with his weathered skin and graying hair. His blue eyes were the one thing she'd inherited from him. Her dark coloring was what she'd gotten from her Hispanic mother.

"This hasn't been my home for a long time." With the aid of her crutch, she bravely made her way into the room.

"You had an accident," Colt said.

"It seems I got in the way at the construction site." She nodded to her ankle. "In a few days

I'll be as good as new. Looks like you're stuck with me for the duration anyway."

"Hap…happy to have you."

His words gave her a strange feeling, making her realize how badly she wanted to be here.

She began to examine the rehab equipment to hide her nervousness. "Looks like I don't need to go to a gym to exercise. You have everything right here."

"You're welcome to u…use it," he told her. "When you're able to."

She sat down on the weight bench and eyed the parallel bars, then Colt. Outside of some weight loss, he looked good. "Is all this helping you?"

He nodded. "Been working hard. I hope to get a lot better s…soon." He studied her. "Thank you for coming home."

That was a first. Her father actually thanked her. "Don't thank me yet. I'm not sure how much I can help, or how long I can stay."

Colt smiled.

Another first, Josie thought, not to mention he was actually carrying on a conversation with her. How many times had she tried to get some attention from this man? She felt tears gathering.

"Just glad you're here," he told her.

Suddenly her throat tightened so she nodded. "I should go and unpack." She got up, slipped the single crutch under her arms and headed for the door, but Colt's gravelly voice made her turn around.

"M...made a lot of mistakes, Josie. I would like a s...second chance."

His words about threw her over the edge. She raised a hand. "I can't deal with any more right now. We'll talk later."

She managed to get out the door and headed toward the staircase. She hopped up the steps on her good leg until she got to the second floor. Using her crutch, she made her way down the familiar hall to the third door on the left that had been her and Tori's bedroom. She stepped inside and froze. It looked the same as it did when she'd left here.

The walls were still pale lavender and the twin beds had floral print comforters with matching dust ruffles. She walked to her bed against the far wall and sank down onto the mattress. Taking a toss pillow from the headboard, she hugged it close against the burning acid in the pit of her stomach.

Great, this trip was supposed to help relax her. This time when tears welled in her eyes she didn't stop them. Colt wanted to rebuild their relationship. What relationship? They'd never had a father/daughter relationship.

Memories of the lonely times welled in her

chest. She'd been grateful for her sisters, especially Tori. When something wonderful happened to them, they'd been each others cheerleaders, along with Kathleen, the housekeeper and their surrogate mom, replacing the mother who'd disappeared from her kids' life when Josie had been only three years old. It had been pretty clear that neither parent wanted their children.

Josie wiped a tear from her cheek. Dang it. She thought she'd gotten over all this. Leaving here and the pain behind, she'd gone off to L.A. and worked hard on a career, building a successful business, Slater Style.

She got up and hobbled to the window and looked out at the ranch compound. From this room, she had a great view of the glossy white barn with the attached corral. There were many outbuildings, some old, plus some new ones that had been added over the years. Her attention turned to the horses grazing in the pasture. There were mares with their foals, frolicking around in the open field.

Smiling, she pressed her hand against the cool glass, knowing cold weather was coming, along with unpredictable Montana snows. Surprisingly, that had been what she'd missed since moving to L.A.

She caught sight of her car coming down the

road and watched as it pulled up in front of the house. Good, she had her vehicle back.

Then she caught sight of two men stepping off the porch below her, Vance and Garrett. She felt a sudden jolt as she got the chance to observe the man she had once called her boyfriend. Both men were about the same height, and drop-dead handsome.

Josie hadn't been surprised at all when she learned Ana and Vance had fallen in love and planned to marry soon. The guy had been crazy about Ana for years, since he'd come to live at the Lazy S when he was a teenager.

She smiled, happy for her sister.

Josie looked back at Garrett. She couldn't help but take notice of the man. He'd filled out since college, and he still had those incredible eyes and sexy smile. And she hated the fact that just seeing him again still had an effect on her. She released a breath, recalling how it felt when he carried her in his arms.

After Vance shook hands with Garrett, her future brother-in-law headed off toward the barn. Garrett went to her car and spoke to the driver, one of the men on his crew.

Then as if Garrett could sense her, he looked up. Their eyes locked, and suddenly she felt her heart pounding in her chest. She finally moved out of his sight and went to lie down on the bed.

What was she doing? She didn't need to re-hash her past. All there was here were the memories of the pain and heartache over her father. Now she also had to deal with Garrett. It had taken her a lot of time to get over him. She'd only been back a few hours and he was already involved in her life again.

Why, after all these years? Normally she never let men distract her, mainly because she hadn't met anyone who could stir her interest. She hadn't met anyone in L.A. she wanted to have a relationship with. She thought about the times she'd tried to find a man. Problem was she'd compared them all to Garrett Temple.

She thought back to the kind and considerate man who'd showed her in so many ways how much he loved her. How Garrett had told her they were going to marry and build a life together after they'd graduated college. Then all too quickly she learned that all those promises were lies when it all came crashing down around them that day....

There was a knock on the door.

She wiped away tears as she rolled over on the bed. "Come in," she called, thinking it was Ana.

The door opened and Garrett stepped inside, carrying her suitcases. "I figured you might need these."

Her heart leaped into her throat. She sat up. "You didn't need to bring my things up."

He set the bags over by the closet. "I told Vance I would. He needed to check on one of his horses."

She nodded. She wasn't sure she believed him. "Thank you."

"How are you feeling?" he asked as he crossed the room.

"I'm fine."

Garrett paused, his gaze searching her face. "I'm sorry I pushed you so hard. I was only trying to get you out of the way." He frowned. "I was worried the truck would hit you."

She nodded. "I should have been paying attention. But I'm fine now, so you can stop feeling guilty."

He still didn't leave. "Some habits are hard to break."

She knew what he was talking about, but their past was the last thing she wanted to rehash. "Well, stop it. I'm a big girl."

He studied her for what seemed to be forever. "Since you're still angry, maybe it's time to clear the air."

"I don't think anything you have to say will change a thing."

He was big and strong, and he seemed to take up a lot of space in the room. "Josie, I don't blame you for not wanting to see me again."

She raised a hand, praying he would just disappear. "I don't want to talk about this, Garrett."

"Well, if you want me to leave then you're going to have to hear me out first."

His gray gaze met hers, causing her pulse to race through her body. Darn the man. "Okay, talk."

"First, I'm sorrier than I can say for what happened all those years ago. I regret that I hurt you. But we broke up, Josie. We hadn't been together all summer, and you wouldn't even talk to me."

Just as it had been all those years ago, Garrett's words were like a knife slicing into her heart. "Feel better now?"

He released a breath. "Although I have many regrets about how things happened between us, what I'll never regret is my son. He's the most important thing in my life."

A son. She had to remember the innocent child. "I'm glad, Garrett. I'm glad you're happy."

He gave a nod. "I just want us to be able to work together on this project."

She wasn't even sure she could stay here. "Is that all?"

He nodded, then turned to leave, but for some reason she needed to know. "Was she worth it?"

Garrett paused and glanced over his shoulder. "I take it you're talking about my wife."

Another pain shot through Josie. "Yes."

"Natalie was my son's mother, so yes, the choice was worth it." She saw the pain flash through his eyes. "But our marriage didn't survive."

The next day at the Temple Ranch, Garrett forced himself out of bed after a sleepless night. Josie Slater was back. He knew he couldn't let her mess with his head, or his heart. Not again.

Why was he even worrying? There was no room for her in his life. So for both their sakes, he hoped she was headed back to California soon.

He walked down the stairs of his father's home. Now, not only had it been Garrett's for the past year, it was Brody's, too. And this morning he'd taken off work from the construction site to spend time with his son. Soon the boy would be starting a new school, so today was going to be just for them. With Brody's recent move to Royerton, he knew it was going to take some time to make the adjustment. And for Garrett to win his son's trust.

Since the divorce two years ago, it had been difficult on his child. Then his ex-wife's recent death in a car accident had struck Brody yet another blow. Garrett hoped that a stable home at the ranch would help the eight-year-old. As his father, he was going to spend as much time as possible with his son now that he was the sole parent.

Garrett finished tucking in his shirt as he walked into the kitchen. He found Brody sitting at the counter, eating a bowl of his favorite cereal.

"Good morning, Brody."

He was rewarded with a big smile. "Morning," his son murmured.

Garrett smiled at the boy who was his image at the same age.

Brody was tall and lanky, with a headful of unruly dark curls and big green eyes. The thing that tore at Garrett's heart was knowing that his son would have struggles without having a mother around. As Brody's father he'd vowed from the day he'd been born that he'd always be there for him.

He walked to the counter and took the mug of coffee from the housekeeper, Della Carlton.

"Thanks, Della." He took a sip. "Sorry I wasn't down earlier, but I needed to phone my crew foreman. How has Brody been this morning?"

"A sweetheart. He does need his routine, though."

Garrett nodded. "Change is hard for all of us."

The short stocky woman had gray hair pulled

up into a ponytail. "It's so wonderful you brought him here. It's been good for your father, too."

Garrett glanced around. "Speaking of Nolan, where is he?"

"Jack Richardson came by and took him to a horse auction."

He frowned, thinking about his father's arthritis. "Dad was up to it?"

Della nodded as they watched Brody carry his bowl to the sink. "The new medication seems to be helping him a lot."

The main reason Garrett had moved back to the ranch was to help out his father. Relocating his construction company took longer, but business was picking up, and with his foreman, Jerry, they could still put in bids on long-distance projects. And now, Brody would be raised here, too.

"Can we go get my horse now?" Brody asked.

Garrett smiled. "Give me a minute."

"Okay. I'm going outside to wait." The boy took off toward the back door.

Garrett glanced at Della. The Temple men were lucky to have her here to help fill in with Brody. "We should be back from the Lazy S by lunch. If plans change I'll call you."

The middle-aged widow nodded. "You just have a good time today."

Garrett knew today Brody would be meeting new people. He'd been so withdrawn since his mother's death. "You think he's ready for his own horse?"

Della smiled. "I'm not an expert, but it seems to me this is the first thing I'd seen the boy get excited about since he's come here to live. I'd say that's a good sign, and isn't horseback riding therapeutic?"

"Dad!" Brody's voice rang out.

"Okay, I'm coming."

"You're doing the right thing by the boy," Della said. "You're a good man, Garrett Temple."

Garrett felt a sudden rush of emotion, but managed a nod. He caught up with his son and headed toward his truck. They were going to see Vance to get a suitable mount.

They climbed in the vehicle, and after buckling up, Garrett drove off toward their closest neighbor.

Since Nolan Temple's health had deteriorated most of the barn stock had been sold off. One of the jobs Garrett had taken on was to get the operation up and going again. Thanks to the ranch foreman, Charlie Bowers, and neighbor Vance Rivers, they now had a herd that was twice the size as last year's, along with an alfalfa crop for the spring.

Even his dad was feeling good enough to want to participate in the operation. Garrett enjoyed it, too, and he hoped the same for his son. He wanted a place where his boy would feel safe and secure again. He wanted that for himself, too.

He glanced at the boy sitting next to him. "Vance has three horses for you to see, but that doesn't mean you have to pick one of them. We can keep looking if you don't find what you want."

Brody shrugged, looking down at his hands. "Okay."

Garrett was eager to get his son something to distract him from the loss of his mother. There had also been some big changes in his life. He just wanted Brody to know that he was his top priority. Not even work was going to distract him from rebuilding a life with his son.

Then he'd seen Josie yesterday.

All these years and she was back here. Seeing her again had been harder than he could imagine. But by her reaction toward him, he didn't have to worry about her being interested in him. Besides, she was probably headed back to California really soon.

Josie had slept in until eight o'clock. After she'd tested the tenderness of her ankle, she managed to shower and rewrapped it. She dressed and was even able to put on a pair of canvas sneakers. Making her way downstairs, she went to the kitchen and was greeted by Kathleen's big smile and hug.

"Where is everyone?"

"Your father is with his therapist, Jay McNeal." The fiftysomething housekeeper glanced at the kitchen clock. "It'll be about another hour. Afterward, Jay helps him shower and get dressed."

"How is Colt really doing? I mean, Ana hadn't given a lot of details." Maybe Josie just hadn't been eager to listen. "Only that he's improving."

"He is improving and very quickly. We're all happy about that." Kathleen sat down across from her. "But your sister still wants your help. She won't ask you to, but she needs you to stay as long as you can spare the time."

Josie felt bad, knowing how much her older sister had taken on by herself. "I should have come sooner."

"Under the circumstances, I can't blame you all for not wanting to come home," she told her. "But I'm sure glad you're here now. Please tell me you're staying awhile." The older woman squeezed her hand. "I missed you, Josie."

"Ah, Kathleen, I've missed you, too." But two weeks was about all she could handle with Garrett. "I said two weeks. After that…" She hesitated. "Remember, Tori is handling my end of the business while I'm here."

"Maybe she'll decide to come back, too."

Josie smiled. "As soon as I get back there, she can come home."

"So you still think of the Lazy S as home?"

Josie shook her head. "Don't start, Kathleen. Let's just take this slow. I've been away a long time." She finished her coffee. "Where's Ana?"

"She went out to the barn with Vance. They have someone coming to look at some horses this morning." Kathleen checked the clock. "Then she had to go to work at the high school."

Josie nodded, knowing the reason she came home was because of Ana's job as high school counselor.

She stood and tested her ankle. "Maybe I'll walk down to have a look around, then come back to see Colt." This was all so new to her. She was actually going to see her dad.

Josie kissed Kathleen's cheek. Grabbing her coat, she headed out the door and slowly made her way down the same path she used to take as a kid. Not that she'd been invited into the barn much. Colt had pretty much kept his daughters out of any ranch business. Even when they got older, he didn't want them around. It had been some of the ranch hands who taught them to rope and ride. When Colt learned of it, he made sure they learned to muck out stalls, too.

She stepped inside the large structure, where

the scent of straw and animals hit her. She smiled, thinking a few days here might not be so bad. She looked down the rows of stalls where several horses were housed. She liked this. Walking down the center aisle, she passed the stall that had the name Blondie on the gate. *Ana's buckskin,* Josie thought as she walked up and began to stroke the animal. Then she went to another stall with a big chestnut, Rusty.

"Well, aren't you a good-looking fella."

"That's Vance's horse."

Josie swung around when she heard a child's voice. She found a boy who was about eight or nine. He must be the buyer's son. "And I bet he's fun to ride, too," she said.

The child didn't make eye contact with her, but he wandered toward her. "Vance says he can chase down calves, too. That's what he's best at."

"We all have to be good at something." Who was this child? "I'm Josie, Ana's sister. And you are?"

"Brody. Vance said my horse can be like Rusty if I train him."

Where was her future brother-in-law? "You have your own horse, Brody?"

Josie watched the child nod, wondering why he looked so familiar. He nodded. "My dad's buying me one. He's brown with a black tail and mane. That means he's a bay. His name is Sky Rocket."

"Cool name."

The child nodded, causing his cowboy hat to tip back. "I'm going to teach him to run really fast."

Josie smiled. "That sounds like a lot of fun."

She was about to say something to the boy when she heard another voice calling out from the other side of the barn. "Brody!"

Josie looked at the boy. "Seems someone is looking for you."

The boy jerked around just as Garrett and Vance came walking down the aisle. "Brody Temple."

Temple. This was Garrett's child. Oh, God, she needed to leave. The last thing she wanted was to see the man again.

"Oh, no," Brody said as he stepped closer to Josie. "My dad is mad."

Suddenly Garrett and Vance came up to them, and she knew she couldn't ditch the boy.

"Brody, you were told not to wander off," his father said. "You're too young to be around horses without someone older."

Suddenly, the kid threw her under the bus. "It's okay. I was with Josie."

CHAPTER THREE

GARRETT WAS BOTH relieved and surprised to find Brody standing beside Josie. His son didn't usually approach strangers.

He looked down at the boy. "Son, you know you can't leave like that."

Brody stiffened. "I was careful," he said defensively, but that changed when Vance walked up to the group. "You sure have a lot of horses here."

"We hope to have a lot more in the spring," Vance said. "So we can keep selling them to other kids." He looked at Josie. "Josie. What brings you out here?"

"I came to find Ana." She looked at the boy and managed to smile. "And found Brody instead."

That smile quickly died when she turned to Garrett. "Seems you spend a lot of time at the Lazy S. I thought you were busy building a lodge."

So she was going to stay angry at him. "I am.

My foreman has everything under control." He placed his hands on Brody's shoulders. "I was taking the morning off to spend with my son. We're picking out his first horse."

"I know. We were talking about Sky Rocket." She sighed. "Look, I should get back to the house to check on Colt. It was nice to meet you, Brody."

Vance stepped in. "Don't go yet, Josie, I was going to show Brody the new foal."

"Yeah, go with us," Brody pleaded.

Garrett knew it was inevitable he'd see Josie, but today he wanted to focus on his son, not his ex-girlfriend.

He could see her indecision, but she finally relented. "I can stay a few minutes."

Brody looked at Vance. "Where is it?"

Grinning, Vance pushed his hat back. "Down a few stalls." They all began walking. Garrett stayed back and let Brody and Josie take the lead, but once they got to the oversize stall, the boy waited, a big grin on his face, until the adults arrived before he got too close. He saw happiness in his child that he hadn't seen in a long time.

Garrett looked over the railing to find a dark chestnut mare. Close by was her pretty brown filly with four white socks just like her mama.

"Oh, she's so little," Brody said as he looked through the stall railings. "How old is she?"

Vance walked up and began to stroke the mare's nose. "Just two weeks."

Josie asked Vance, "Do you think the mama will let us pet her?"

Garrett enjoyed seeing the light in her eyes, the excitement in her voice. It had been a long time since he'd seen this carefree side of Josie.

"Sure. Sugar Plum is a sweetheart." He opened the gate, went inside and nudged the mare back and stood in front of her so the group could see the long-legged filly.

"So what do you think of her, Brody?" Vance asked.

Garrett knelt down away from the new mother, then reached out a hand to coax the filly, turning to Brody. "Come here, son."

The boy walked inside the stall and mimicked his dad. "She's so little."

His son seemed to have no fear of animals as he reached out his hand to the foal. Surprisingly, the horse sniffed it and allowed the boy to touch her. Brody grinned. "She likes me. Josie, she likes me."

Josie moved in next to Brody. "Animals are trusting as long as you don't hurt them."

Garrett couldn't take his eyes off the exchange between his son and the foal, also between Josie and Brody. He felt a tightening in his chest. Josie always had an easy way, a knack to make people feel comfortable.

Josie stood up and let Brody interact with the foal. There was a bond growing already. She glanced at Garrett, seeing the love and protectiveness he had for his child. She felt tears welling in her eyes as she thought about past regrets. What could have been if only... She quickly blinked them away.

"Hey, Brody," Vance said. "Can you think of a name for our filly?"

The child shrugged. "I don't know any names for a horse."

Josie saw the boy begin to withdraw. "Maybe," she suggested, "'cause her mom's name is Sugar Plum, you can call her 'Sweet' something." She shrugged. "You know, like Sweet Pea. Sweet Georgia Brown. Sweet Caroline. Sweetheart. Sweet Potato."

"Sweet potato?" Brody giggled. "That's a silly name."

"Well, come up with something better," she told him.

The child continued to stroke the animal. "How about Sweet as Sugar," he said. "My mom used to say that to me when I was little." His voice faded out. "Before she died."

Oh, God. Josie's heart nearly stopped as she

shot a look at Garrett. He didn't make eye contact with her. His gaze stayed on his child as he went to the boy. "I think your mom would really like that name."

Vance spoke up. "I think that's a perfect name. It's got her mother's name in it, too. We'll call her Sweetie for short. How do you like that, Sugar?" The horse whinnied and bobbed her head.

Brody flashed a big grin and his green eyes sparkled.

Josie felt a tug at her heart. "Yeah. That's a good name. Sweetie."

Vance patted the mare's neck as he winked at Josie. "Thank you. Good idea."

"Anytime, soon-to-be brother-in-law." She smiled and glanced at Garrett. He was watching her, and she felt the familiar feelings, that warm shiver as his gaze locked on hers. She hated that he still had an effect on her, but she refused to let him see it. "I should get back to the house and Colt."

"We all need to leave," Garrett said. "The mama has been patient long enough with her visitors."

Brody stood up. "Bye, Sweetie. Bye, Sugar."

After the stall gate closed, Josie turned to the child. "It was nice to meet you, Brody."

"Nice meeting you, Josie," the boy said, then

when she started to walk out, he asked shyly, "Will I see you again?"

She was caught off guard. "Oh, probably. We're neighbors. And your dad is building a lodge for us."

"I know. My dad builds a lot of stuff."

She smiled, trying desperately to get away. "Enjoy your new horse." She stole a look at Garrett. "Goodbye." She tried not to run out of the barn, not that her sore ankle would allow it anyway.

Twenty-four hours home, and this man had been everywhere she turned. She knew one thing. She needed to get out of Montana as soon as possible.

She didn't need Garrett Temple messing up her life…again.

An hour later, Josie sat at the desk in her father's office talking on the phone with Tori. "How did the meeting go with Reed Corp?" she asked her sister, who'd pretty much taken over Josie's event business while she was here.

"It went well. They were disappointed that you weren't at the presentation. I think Jason Reed has a thing for you."

Josie shook her head. "He also has a wife and two kids." The short, balding fortysomething man liked all women. "I don't share well, remember?"

She glanced around Colt's private domain as she listened to her sister. The den walls were done in a dark wood paneling, and against one of those walls was a floor-to-ceiling bookcase filled with books, old rodeo buckles and trophies along with blue ribbons for Lazy S's award-winning cattle and horses.

The furniture was worn leather and the carpet needed to be replaced. How long had the ranch finances been bad?

Tori's laughter came over the speakerphone. "That's right, you were pretty stingy when we were growing up, not sharing your dolls or your boyfriend. Speaking of which, how is Garrett?"

Josie froze. Why did everything come back to that man? "How would I know?"

"Because Ana said you've been spending time with him."

"That's not by choice."

"So how does he look? Please tell me he's gotten fat and gone bald."

Josie had only confided in her twin what really happened the day Garrett confessed that he'd planned to marry another woman. Later she'd learned he'd gotten her pregnant. "No, he pretty much looks the same."

"Ana also told me that he's moved back to

the Temple Ranch with his son." Tori paused. "If you want, Josie, you can come back to L.A., and I'll take your place."

"No, I can't keep running away from my past. We both decided that we'd help Ana and Vance. Besides, I want to find out if Colt's new attitude toward his daughters is for real."

"You have doubts?"

Josie wasn't sure, still leery of the man's sudden change of heart. "He's nothing like the man we remember, Tori. He actually talked to me this morning at breakfast. Since the man had pretty much ignored us when we were growing up, I'm not sure how to handle the new Colt Slater."

Tori joined in. "Like I said, we can change places if you want to come back here."

Josie was a little worried. Why was Tori so eager to come to Montana? "Is there something you're not telling me?"

"No, I've just been working a lot of hours."

"You're being careful, aren't you? Have you heard from Dane again?"

"No."

Tori's ex-boyfriend, Dane Buckley, had abused her. Josie shivered, recalling the night her sister had showed up on her doorstep with the bruises and busted lip. When she wanted to call the police, Tori begged her not to, not wanting anyone to know. They'd settled on getting a restraining order.

"You need to call Detective Brandon if Dane comes anywhere near you."

She heard the hesitation. "What aren't you telling me?"

"It's just a feeling… Dane's around. I saw a car like his down the street by the town house."

Josie leaned her arms on the deck, fighting her anger. "Then tell that to the detective. He can check around to make sure you're safe. That's their job."

"Okay, I will."

"No, I mean it, Tori. You don't want to take any chances with that jerk."

Josie looked up and saw Garrett standing in the doorway. She quickly picked up the receiver, taking the phone off speaker. "Just listen to me about this. Please, promise me."

She heard the exaggerated sigh. "I said I would. Right after I hang up I'll call Detective Brandon."

"Good. I better go, but could you send your samples for the lodge's website design?"

"Sure. Bye, Josie."

"Bye, Tori." She hung up the phone and looked across the room at the man who seemed to be everywhere she was. "Is there a problem, Garrett?"

"I was about to ask you the same thing," he said. "Is Tori all right?"

Josie shrugged. "She's fine."

Garrett walked to the desk. "Look, Josie, if someone is stalking your sister, it's serious. Maybe I can help."

Josie didn't want to talk to Garrett about this, or anything else. "Thank you, but we have it under control."

Garrett watched for a moment, and then finally nodded. "Okay, but the offer stands."

"Fine. So what brings you here?"

"I just got a call from my foreman from the lodge. He has questions about the bathroom locations."

Josie shook her head. "I have nothing to do with that. You need to ask Ana."

"I would, but Ana's not available. She's tied up in meetings all day and can't get away. If you want to keep this project on schedule, the rough plumbing problems need to get resolved before any walls go up."

"Fine. The last thing I want is any delays." She stood. She found she was excited about getting involved in the project. She'd always been a natural-born organizer. She just didn't want to spend any time with Garrett. "How soon do you need me there?"

"Right now. I can drive you out, but Brody

will be going with us. Then I can come back here to trailer his horse."

Josie hated the idea, but what choice did she have? "Okay." She grabbed her jacket off the back of the chair. She headed out, but Garrett's voice stopped her.

"Brody's in the kitchen. Kathleen is feeding him some lunch."

Josie felt her own stomach protest from lack of food. "That's not a bad idea. I could use some nourishment."

They walked down the hall to the bright kitchen and heard laughter. At the big table sat Brody and her father. Kathleen was at the stove stirring a pot of soup. "Sit down, you two," the housekeeper said. "And I'll fix you something to eat."

Colt looked up at them, as did the boy. Both smiled mischievously.

"Hey, Dad, did you know that Colt used to be a World Saddle Bronc champion?"

Garrett nodded. Who would have thought, gruff, strictly business Colton Slater could make his son smile?

"I might have heard it somewhere." He nodded at the older man across from his son. "Hello, Colt. How are you doing these days?"

Colt looked at Josie. "Not bad. T...two of my daughters are home."

"Colt's learning to talk again," Brody explained. "'Cause he had a stroke. But he's getting better."

Garrett sat down at the table. "That's good news." He looked at Colt. "Did Brody tell you we just bought one of your horses?"

"Yeah, Sky Rocket," Brody said. "I'm going to learn to ride him really fast."

Colt frowned. "I'm s…sure you are. But f… first you have to learn to take care of your animal so he'll trust you."

A confused Brody looked at his dad.

"It means when you get an animal you have to take responsibility for it. You need to feed and clean up after Rocket."

He glanced back at Colt, his green eyes worried. "But I'm just a kid."

Kathleen brought two more bowls of potato soup to the table. Josie reluctantly took her seat beside her father.

"You'll learn some now, and as you get older you'll do more," Garrett told him. "You live on a ranch now. That means everyone does their share."

Brody took a hearty spoonful of soup, then said, "If I do all that stuff, will you teach me how to ride a bucking bronc?"

Colt watched out the window as the threesome drove off to the lodge site. He had to admit that he'd enjoyed sharing lunch with them.

"See, that wasn't so bad, was it?" Kathleen said. "Too bad you didn't get cozier with your kids a lot sooner."

Colt turned and made his way back to the kitchen table, but didn't say anything. Nothing to say. He'd messed up big-time when it came to his girls.

Kathleen placed two mugs filled with coffee on the table, then sat down across from him. "Looks like you're getting another chance at being their dad. I hope you realize how lucky you are."

Colt hated that it had taken him so many years to learn that. He thought about his girls. Why had it taken him so long to realize what they meant to him? Josie was home, but so was Garrett Temple. How was she handling seeing him again? He recalled how badly she'd been hurt by their breakup. Now Garrett had returned and brought his son with him. He could see being around the man bothered Josie, in more ways than he knew his daughter would ever admit.

"Did you see Josie with Garrett?"

Kathleen set down her mug. "That girl has a lot of you in her. If Garrett comes sniffing around again, I doubt she's going to make it easy for him." She shook her head. "Of course that little boy has to come first. From what I hear from Della, Brody's had a rough few years with the divorce and lately with his mother's death."

Colt nodded. "A horse would be good for him."

Kathleen smiled. "And maybe some time with you. He sure didn't have any trouble talking with you."

Colt would always regret that he never took time to console his own daughters. He couldn't get past his own anger. "Sometimes it's easier with strangers."

Thirty minutes later, Josie sat in the front seat as Garrett pulled his truck into his makeshift parking area at the site. He pulled his hard hat off the dashboard, then reached in the back and found one for Brody, then another for Josie.

"Keep these on for your safety," he told them both.

"Good idea," Josie said and put it on. "Let's go check out this place." She climbed out as Garrett opened the back door and helped Brody out.

Even though the circumstances weren't ideal, she was eager to see the lodge. She pulled her coat together against the chill and waited for Brody and Garrett to catch up to her.

Together, they walked across the wet ground

to the sheets of plywood covering the mud caused by last night's rain.

They reached the front door. Well, it was where the door was going to be. This was still a two-story log cabin shell. The outside logs were up, along with the roof, but not much more. She inhaled the scent of fresh-cut wood as they walked through the wide doorway into what would be the main meeting room. More like an open area with high ceilings of tongue-and-groove oak.

Josie glanced around at the huge picture windows that overlooked the river. Drawn to the beautiful scenery, she walked over. This was a perfect spot. In her head, she was already figuring out different events that could be held here.

The first was the Slater/Rivers wedding right in front of these windows. She began to visualize the number of chairs that the room could handle, leaving room for an aisle. She turned to the men working on the floor-to-ceiling fireplace made out of river rock. It took her breath away.

"How do you like it so far?"

She swung around to see Garrett and Brody. She couldn't help but smile. "It's really nice. In fact, it's better than I thought possible. There's a lot we can do with this space. Are the floors going to be hardwood?"

When Garrett nodded, she looked toward

the roughed-in stairs to the second floor. It was going to be left open, a mezzanine level for the bedrooms upstairs. She hated that anglers would be using it. She could really promote this for high-dollar functions.

"Okay, I see your mind working," Garrett said. "Tell me what it is."

Josie turned toward him. "It would be nice if we didn't have to use it for anglers."

Garrett arched an eyebrow. "Before we open to the public there's going to be a wedding here."

She tensed, recalling when she was planning her own wedding, until her groom betrayed her.

She wiped the picture from her mind. "I know. I'll go over those details with Ana." She released a breath. "Okay, where are these bathrooms that need my attention?"

He glanced around. "I need to find Jerry."

When Garrett went off to find the foreman, Josie realized she had to find a way to get over her resentment toward him. It would be the only way this project would get completed.

Her cell phone rang and she reached inside her purse to answer it. "Hello."

"Josie, it's Ana."

"Hey, Ana. Are you planning to come out to the site?"

"No. I'm at the house, but we need to discuss the lodge."

"What about it?" she asked, and walked away from the group.

"I found out today that I'm going to a teacher's conference in Helena," Ana told her. "The school principal is sick and he asked me to take his place. I have to go out of town for three days."

Three days. She looked at Garrett talking with the foreman. "You're leaving me here alone?"

Ana paused. "I'm not doing this on purpose, Josie. It's only for a few days. Since you helped with the building plans, I figured this should be easy."

Josie glanced across the room. She was going to have to spend more time with Garrett. Hadn't she already been doing that over the past twenty-four hours?

"Come on, I've seen you organize and delegate," Ana said. "This will be easy."

What could she say? "Okay, have a safe trip. But expect a lot of phone calls, because I'm still going to need your help."

"You've got Garrett."

That was what she was afraid of. Already her stomach began to hurt. She said goodbye and hung up as Garrett walked over.

"Is there something wrong?" he asked.

"Ana has to go out of town. Looks like you're stuck working with me."

A smile twitched at the corners of his mouth. "I can handle it, but can you?"

She wanted to wipe that smile off his face. "This is business. I can handle it with ease." Garrett Temple, the man, she wasn't so sure.

CHAPTER FOUR

GARRETT COULD SEE how hard Josie worked to hold her temper, but the frown lines between her eyes, and her clenched hands gave her away.

"Hey, don't be angry at me. I didn't send Ana out of town."

"I didn't say you did. I'm just saying, I'm not that sure about what's going on here at the site."

He glanced around at the work going on. "I don't believe that. Wasn't this lodge your idea?"

"A general idea is far from making decisions on the design," she argued. "Shouldn't you be doing that?"

"I could, but in order to save money on this project, your sister was going to handle that."

Before she could say anything, Brody walked toward him.

"Hey, Dad, Jerry said if it's all right with you he'll take me to look at the bulldozer. Can I go, please?"

Garrett glanced at his foreman to see him give

the thumbs-up. Since Jerry had three of his own kids, he knew that his son would be taken care of.

"Sure. Just do what Jerry says." He tapped his son's head. "And keep your hard hat on."

"Okay," the boy yelled as he shot off toward Jerry.

Garrett turned back to Josie. She still wasn't happy. "Come on, let's go upstairs so we can discuss this in private." He grabbed her hand, surprised that she didn't fight to get it back.

He led her through the crew working on the inside walls, then up the makeshift steps to the second story.

"Be careful," he told her. Once on the plywood floor upstairs, he still didn't let go of her small hand. Even with the flood of memories that reminded him how easily he could get mixed up with Josie Slater again, he held on tight to her hand.

Once safely on solid ground, he released her hand and went over to his plumber, Pete Saunders. "Hey, Pete, how's it going?"

The stocky-built man turned around, and seeing Josie, he smiled. "Hey, Garrett."

"Pete, this is Ana's sister Josie Slater. Josie, Pete."

She nodded. "Hi, Pete. I hear you have some problems."

"Well, not exactly problems, but more or less, a design issue. I'd rather get it right the first time than have to redo any work. It saves time and money."

"A man after my own heart." Josie smiled at him, and the plumber smiled back. "So, Pete, what do you need from me?"

"Well, there are four bedrooms upstairs. Each has its own bath." Pete walked her through a framed room and into a smaller area. "This is one of the bath spaces." He pushed his hard hat back. "My question is, do we put in bathtubs with showers, or a tub with a separate shower stall? I know that most fishermen could care less about a tub, but you want this lodge to be multifunctional. So I thought you should be the one to choose."

Garrett watched Josie, and without missing a beat, she said, "We definitely are going for the bigger clientele base here. They'll want a retreat." She glanced at Garrett. "I know we're trying to save on the budget, but since we're hoping to add on to the structure later on, I feel the upgrades would be a good investment now."

Garrett gave her a nod, agreeing, too.

Josie turned back to Pete then pointed to where everything was going. "So, a spa tub here, then a separate double shower with several sprays, here and here. Can you get in a vanity with two sinks?"

Garrett didn't hear anything else after double shower, big enough for two people—lovers. He glanced at Josie in her slim jeans and turtleneck sweater that showed off her curves. The picture quickly reminded him that he hadn't been with a woman in a long time. He'd been divorced for two years. His dating life had been virtually nonexistent because he wanted to spend as much time as possible with his son.

Now he'd been thrown together with the one woman who could cause him to regret what he'd been missing.

"Garrett, what do you think?" Josie asked. "Is there money in the budget for what I want?"

Get your head back on business. "What? Oh, I think so. If you shop for some good bargains on the fixtures and cabinets, the budget can handle it."

Josie looked thoughtful. He could see her mind working. She was no doubt planning out her strategy to get the job done. It seemed she wasn't thinking about going back to California just yet. Great. Just what he needed—another complication in his life right now.

Two hours later, after a complete tour of the lodge, and going over the progress and building details, Garrett drove Josie back to the house. Was it her, or did it seem easier to talk to him? At least when the subject was business. She only hoped that she didn't physically need to be by the man's side to make more decisions.

Garrett pulled up and stopped in front of the house. Josie reached for the door handle and paused to say, "If you'll point me in the direction of the wholesale plumbing house I'll go see what I can find."

"I'll come up with a list of places. We have some time before they're needed."

With a nod, Josie looked in the backseat at Brody. "Have fun with Sky Rocket, Brody."

The boy didn't look happy. "I can't because I have to start school."

Josie smiled. "Oh, that's good. You'll make all kinds of new friends there. It's a nice school."

"Is that where you knew my dad?"

Josie felt the heat move up her neck. "Yes, we were friends, but it was a long time ago."

Brody looked at his dad. "Was that before you knew Mom?"

Josie's breath caught as she glanced at Garrett. She could see he was uncomfortable with the question. Good.

"Yes, I knew Josie in high school." He rested his hand on the steering wheel. "I played football and she was a cheerleader. When we got older we used to go out with other friends, too." Garrett grinned. "If my memory serves me, Josie used to like to dance and sing karaoke."

She gasped. How could he remember that? "That was one time," she told him. "And as I recall, I did it on a dare."

He continued to smile, knowing he'd been the culprit.

She glanced at Brody again. "Give me some time and I'll tell you stories about your dad that will make you laugh your head off."

She got a smile from the kid. "Oh, boy," he said.

"I've got to go now." Josie waved. "Bye, Brody and Garrett." She opened the door and climbed out, knowing she couldn't get chummy with Garrett Temple and his son. No matter how cute, or how charming. It would lead nowhere.

She headed up the steps, opened the front door and walked inside to see her father coming out of his downstairs bedroom. He was using a cane today.

"Well, look at you. You seem to be getting around like a pro."

He stopped and waited for her. "It's all the great nursing."

They started a slow walk toward the kitchen. She was surprised he was doing so well. "It's good that you're recovering so fast."

"And th...thank you for coming home to help." He paused. "I gave you plenty of reasons never to come back here. I'm sorry."

Whoa. This was too much to handle. "Is the apology for bringing me here now, or for all the years you ignored your daughters?"

"F...for all the above. I know there isn't anything I can do to change the past, but if p...possible, I want to try and change how things are between us now."

Josie tried to speak, but emotions swamped her.

"It's okay." Colt put his hand on her arm. "I don't expect an answer, or your trust. I just want a chance to get to know you while you're here."

Josie nodded and went into the kitchen. Kathleen was preparing supper. "Hey, you two, what are you up to?"

"Just talkin'," Colt said.

Josie walked to the large bay window that overlooked the barn, where Garrett's truck was hooked to the horse trailer. She eyed the man as he led Sky Rocket to the ramp and up into the trailer. Brody stood by and watched as his father latched the gate, then he placed his hand on his son's shoulder and helped him into the truck.

"Nice boy."

Josie didn't turn when she heard her father.

"He's had a rough time," Josie said.

"Seems they both have," Colt answered.

Josie gave her father a sideways glance. "He brought on his troubles himself."

"I know. He hurt you badly. I wish I could have protected you all those years ago."

It surprised her that her father had known what happened. "I wish you'd have been there, too," she admitted.

She'd hurt more than she could tell anyone. More than she ever wanted to remember. But Garrett hadn't been the only man in her life to hurt her.

Monday morning Garrett drove Brody to school. He wanted to take his son on his first day. He glanced down at his solemn-looking eight-year-old. Six months ago when Natalie was killed in the automobile accident, he let his ex-in-laws keep the boy while he finished his move from Butte to Royerton. Although he'd visited Brody as much as possible, he knew that the move would be difficult for the boy. His son had to leave his home, friends and grandparents to move to a new place. That was tough for a kid, especially a kid who'd recently lost his mother.

"Look, Brody, being the new kid in school is never easy, but Royerton is your home now. It's a new start for both of us."

"But I liked my old school."

"I know, but I couldn't stay there. Grandpa Nolan needs us here to help with the ranch."

He pulled into the parking lot and they got out and walked toward the large complex that housed the community's school-aged children from kindergarten through eighth grade. The other building was the high school.

Standing in front of the elementary building was Brody's new teacher, Miss Lisa Kennedy. She looked about eighteen. Garrett had met with her last week, and was confident that she would do everything possible to help his son adjust to his new school.

"Mr. Temple," she said with a smile as she looked at Brody. "Good morning, Brody. I'm so happy that you'll be joining my class."

"Morning, Miss Kennedy," he murmured.

She kept eye contact with Brody. "I know it's tough starting a new school, so Royerton Elementary started the buddy system. And I have someone who's been anxious to meet you." The teacher looked toward the playground and motioned to someone. A small, redheaded boy about eight years old came running to them. "Brody, this is Adam Graves. Adam, meet Brody."

"Hi, Brody," Adam said. "You're going to be in my class." The freckled-faced boy smiled. "I was new last year, so I wanted to be the buddy this year."

Brody didn't say anything.

The boy looked at his teacher and when he got a nod, he said, "I hear you got a new horse."

The question got his son's attention. "Yeah, Sky Rocket. Do you have a horse?"

Adam shook his head. "Not anymore because we moved into town. But when my dad was around, I used to have a pony, Jodie."

Brody studied the boy. "Hey, maybe...you can come out to my house and see Sky Rocket sometime." He glanced up at his father. "Can he, Dad?"

Garrett felt a weight lift on seeing his child's enthusiasm. "Sure. Maybe after I talk with Adam's mother." He wanted to make sure he followed the right protocol for playdates. "Right now I think Miss Kennedy wants you to go to class."

The pretty teacher nodded as the bell rang. "Adam, why don't you take Brody to the classroom and show him where his desk is?"

"Okay, Miss Kennedy. Come on, Brody."

"Bye, Dad." Brody took off with his new friend.

"Bye, son. Have a good day," he called, but knew Brody wasn't hearing him. That was a good thing, right?

"He's going to be fine, Mr. Temple."

He nodded. "I know, but it's been a rough few

months." It had been for him, too. He hadn't known how to handle his son's sadness.

"I'll call you if there are any problems."

"Thank you." Garrett walked off toward his truck and grabbed the lodge plans off the seat. Since he was here, he could catch Ana up on the progress and see if he could steal her for a few hours to help him with some design decisions.

He walked across the same school yard that a dozen years ago he once attended, and memories flooded back. He'd liked school. He had friends and was a good student. The girls liked him, too. But on that first day of his junior year when he walked though the front doors and literally ran into the new freshman, Josefina Slater, he was a goner.

He'd known the Slater sisters all his life, but that summer something changed with her. Josie's eyes were a richer blue, her face was prettier, and her body… Oh, God, her body.

He shivered, recalling how beautiful she looked. If only she still didn't have that effect on him.

He pulled open the door to the high school, and was quickly brought back to the present when he was nearly knocked over by a rush of teenagers.

Garrett removed his cowboy hat and headed to the office as his thoughts returned to Josie.

He had to stop thinking about her because nothing could start up between them.

Not that she wanted anything to do with him. What they once had, had to stay a fond memory. He needed to concentrate on the future. Brody needed him full-time and so did his dad.

He opened the door and smiled at the receptionist, Clare Stewart. He remembered her from school. Of course, in a town of six thousand people, everyone knew most of the citizens.

"Hey, Garrett, it's been a few years."

He shook her hand. "Hello, Clare. It's good to see you again."

"So what brings you to the principal's office?"

"I'm not here to see the principal, but Ana Slater. Is she in her office?"

The pretty blonde shook her head. "No, she's in there." She pointed to the door that read Principal.

"Is she in a meeting?"

"No, she's with her sister, Josie." Clare raised an eyebrow. "You remember Josie, don't you?"

Garrett didn't answer. Everyone in school pretty much knew that they'd been a couple. With Josie's return home, no doubt there would be gossip around town. He knocked on the door and opened it to find the two Slater sisters in a heated discussion.

Josie swung around and glared at him. "What are you doing here?"

So much for getting along, he thought. He ignored her and closed the door behind him. "I came to see Ana, but good, I got both of you."

The last person Josie wanted in on this discussion was Garrett. She wanted to walk out, but she knew it wasn't the professional thing to do. She counted to ten to calm her racing pulse, then asked, "Did you need something?"

"Yeah, a project manager." He looked from Ana to her. "There needs to be someone around to make the decisions."

Ana turned to Josie. *Oh, no, this wasn't going to land in her lap.* "I thought I answered your questions Friday," she told Garrett.

"There are still more decisions to make. If either of you could stop by the site daily so there aren't any holdups that would be nice. When I have to chase down someone, it causes delays and costs money."

Josie turned to her sister. "Well, Ana?"

Her older sister shook her head. "Josie, I explained to you already." She then turned to Garrett. "My principal is in the hospital with pneumonia. I've been asked to take his place for the next few weeks. I've already taken so much time off as it is, and with my wedding coming…"

Ana sighed. "I'm sorry, Garrett. I never planned for this to happen. Like I was trying to tell Josie, I need her to take my place on the project."

"And I've told you, I'm not going to be in town that long," Josie shot back.

Josie could see Garrett was losing patience. "Seems that's been your tune since you've arrived here. Fine, you want me to have all the control? I can make the decisions and the hell with you wanting your corporate retreat."

He turned and started for the door. Curse that man. "Hold up there, Temple."

Garrett stopped and waited for her to speak.

"Are you headed out there now?" she asked.

Garrett nodded. "Yeah, I just dropped Brody off at school."

Josie walked toward him. "Okay, but I don't have my car. I needed to get my brakes fixed. I'll have to ride out with you, but that also means you'll have to drop me off at the ranch." She'd get one of the men to bring her back to town later to get her car from Al's Garage.

After saying goodbye to Ana, Josie hurried to get outside. The air was downright cold today. She pulled her sweater coat tighter.

"You're going to need a warmer coat if you stay around much longer. My dad's predicting an early winter."

At the mention of Nolan Temple, Josie got all soft inside. "How is your Dad?"

"He's been doing better on this new medication, but his arthritis gets worse in the colder weather."

They reached his truck, and Garrett opened the passenger door, but he knew better than to help her in. A flash of memory took him back to how he used to swing the teenage Josie up in his arms and set her down on the seat. He used to be rewarded with a kiss.

A sudden ache constricted his chest as he watched her climb into the pickup. She did just fine without him, like she had for all these years. Maybe that had been their problem, her stubborn independence.

After he shut the door, he hurried around to the other side and got in behind the wheel. He immediately started up the engine and turned on the heat. The soft sounds of country-Western music filled the cab. He caught a whiff of her scent. It was the same perfume she'd worn years ago.

He needed a distraction. "Are you up for a drive into Butte?"

She looked at him, her eyes leery. "Why?"

"I thought we could pick out the bathroom and kitchen tiles along with the sinks and tubs. We can get it out of the way now…before you have to go back to California." He checked his watch. "I have until three o'clock when I pick up Brody from school."

She hesitated as their gazes locked. It seemed to be a battle of wills. Even years ago, Josie liked to be in control. "Sure."

Hiding his surprise, Garrett put the truck in gear and pulled out onto Main Street and headed for the highway out of town. "You know this working together would be so much easier if you weren't always ready to fight me all the time."

She didn't say anything.

"Josie, what happened between us was a long time ago. I'm not saying you have to like me, but can't we put what happened aside? We were kids. It's time to move on."

"You're right, Temple. I need to think about the River's Edge project and nothing else." She glared at him as he turned onto the highway. "But that doesn't mean we can be friends."

Her words hurt him more than he wanted to admit. At one time, Josie Slater had been his best friend and his girl. They shared everything, but then that summer everything changed and not for the good.

"I'm sorry to hear that, Josie."

By noon, Josie was enjoying herself. They'd gone to a builders supply house and looked over cabinets and sinks for the kitchen and baths. She also realized that Garrett had good taste when it came to colors for tiles and flooring. The store's designer, Diana, was more than willing to help them. The way she looked at Garrett, Josie suspected the two had more than a business relationship. She hated that the other woman's attention toward Garrett bothered her.

After the order had been placed and a delivery date set, they walked back out to the truck.

"You seem to be well-known around here," she said.

"I built my construction company in this area. It's a good idea to be nice to everyone because most of my work is from word of mouth. I worked years to build a good reputation and I've done most of my trade here."

They climbed in the truck. "So why did you move everything back to Royerton?"

"Dad. He can't handle the ranch on his own." He released a breath. "And since my divorce and only getting to see Brody twice a week, I could spend more time at the ranch."

Josie didn't want to talk about his marriage. It wouldn't matter anyway. Garrett had given up on her years ago.

"How is the business since moving to Royerton?"

Garrett stopped at the light and glanced at her.

"Not bad. I'm lucky that my foreman is willing to bid on jobs here in Butte. My crew is pretty mobile and they'll go almost anywhere for work."

Garrett drove down the street, then pulled his truck into the parking lot of the local café and shut off the engine. "Come on, I'll buy you some lunch."

He got out before she could argue. Since she was hungry, she didn't put up a fight. She hurried to catch up with him. Okay, so he was treating her like one of the guys. Wasn't that what she wanted him to do?

He stopped at the entrance and held open the door. She went inside first and glanced around the mom-and-pop place, with ruffled curtains and floral wallpaper.

"They've got the best food around." He smiled as an older woman came over. "Hi, Dolly."

The fortysomething woman looked at him and smiled. "Well, well, if it isn't Garrett Temple. Where is that sweet boy of yours?"

Garrett removed his cowboy hat. "He's in school in Royerton."

She moved across the café, her blond ponytail swinging back and forth. "So you got him settled in?"

"I'm trying. He's still a little sad about the move."

"He's lucky to have you." The woman turned to Josie. "Hi, I'm Dolly Madison." She raised a hand. "I've heard every joke there is. And if that guy cooking in the kitchen there wasn't about perfect, I wouldn't have married him and put up with the headache."

Josie smiled. "Nice to meet you, Dolly. I'm Josie Slater."

"Welcome to Dolly's Place." She grabbed two menus and led them to a table in the corner. Once they were seated, Dolly brought over two mugs of coffee, and the busboy filled their water glasses. After they ordered a club sandwich and a hamburger, Dolly left them alone.

Josie looked at him. She hated that she was so curious about Garrett's past. "You seem to have a nice life here."

His gray eyes were distant. "It's funny how looks can be deceiving."

Later that night, Colt had retired to his room, but he couldn't sleep. He thought about Josie and how quiet she'd been at supper. She had started to open up, to talk to him, but tonight she was quiet again. He knew she'd spent the day with Garrett. Had something happened between them?

He fought to keep from phoning the Temple Ranch and having a word with the man. Colt stood and went to the window and looked out into the night. The security lights were on, so he could see all the way to the barn and into the empty corral.

It was all quiet.

Problem was he wanted to be the one who did the last walk through the barn to check on the horses.

So many things had changed in the past few months. Two daughters had come home, one was engaged to marry. He smiled at the thought of Vance officially becoming a part of the family. Vance Rivers was a good man.

Colt sobered. If he wasn't careful, he could lose another daughter. Josie just might head back to California if she decided she couldn't deal with her past.

He knew everything about dealing with his past. He still couldn't let go of their mother. Lucia had nearly destroyed him. He walked slowly back to his bed and sat down. He worked the buttons on his Western-cut shirt and then pulled it off. He kicked off slippers, and couldn't wait until he was sure-footed enough to put on his well-broken-in Justin boots again. He stood and stripped down his jeans. He managed it all without Jay's help. He might not get to cowboy much these days, but he still liked to dress like one.

He turned off the bedside light, pulled back

the blanket and got in. He laid his head against the pillow and stared at the outside lights making a pattern on the ceiling.

He shut his eyes as the familiar loneliness washed over him. He'd had the same feelings for a lot of years, but hard work helped him fight off the worst times. He closed his eyes, hoping sleep would take it away.

He must have dozed off when he heard the pocket door to his room open. It was probably one of the girls checking on him. When the figure moved to the bed, he caught a whiff of her fragrance. His eyes opened and his breath caught. "Lucia…"

"Yes, *mi amor.* I am here," she said, her voice soft and throaty. Her hand reached out and touched his face. Colt shivered as he looked at the woman he'd given his heart to so many years ago. Her face was in the shadows, but he saw the silhouette, the delicate features and the black hair that caressed her shoulders.

He knew it was her. His Lucia.

He blinked several times to get a better look, but his eyes grew heavy and he couldn't keep them open any longer. He didn't fight it, not wanting to disturb this wonderful dream.

CHAPTER FIVE

IT WAS ABOUT six the next morning when Josie awoke to the sound of voices outside her bedroom. She got up, realized how cold it was and pulled her sweatshirt over her head then went to the door.

Outside in the hall were Ana and Vance. "Hey, what's going on?" She rubbed the sleep from her eyes. "Is there a fire or something?"

The twosome didn't smile.

"Sorry to disturb you, sis," Ana began, "but Vance needs to move the herd in from the north pasture."

"There's a blizzard headed our way," Vance added. "And we're going to need every willing body we can get our hands on to help." He glanced over her pajama-clad body. "Think you're able to ride with us?"

Ana gasped. "Vance, no. Josie hasn't been on a horse in years. And it's cold out there."

Vance grinned. "So our California girl can't take the Montana cold?"

The two were talking and leaving her out. "Hey, I can speak for myself."

They both looked at her. "I remember how to ride, and if someone loans me a pair of long johns and a heavy coat, sure I'll join you."

"No, Josie. It's not safe."

"Ana, you'd be riding out if you weren't needed at the school."

Ana started to argue, then said, "You're right, but if this storm is as bad as they say, the high school will be shut down tomorrow. So I need to go in today. But I want you to take Blondie. She's a good mount and knows how to work cattle." She glanced at her soon-to-be husband. "You better take care of her, or you'll be moving back into the barn."

Josie left the couple to finish the argument and went into the shower. When she got back to her bedroom, she found thermal underwear, a winter coat, scarf and gloves on the bed and fur-lined boots next to the chair.

Josie dressed quickly, then went down to the kitchen, where she found Colt and Kathleen at the table.

"Hey, I hear there's a storm coming," she said as she poured some coffee.

Her father turned to her. "I wish you didn't have to go out in it. I sh…should go."

She sat down and began to eat the plate of

eggs Kathleen put in front of her. "You will. Just keep getting better, and the next blizzard is yours."

She watched as a smile appeared on his face. Her chest grew tight and her eyes filled. Colt Slater smiling?

"That's a deal, but I'd like you to ride with me."

This was killing her. "If you get back on a horse, then I'll go with you." Why did it matter so much that her dad wanted to go riding with her? "Deal?"

Colt's blue gaze met hers as she stuck out her hand. "Deal."

They finished breakfast in silence, and she put on her coat, wrapped the scarf around her neck and chin and hurried out to the barn. She found Vance had finished loading four horses into a trailer.

Once finished, he gave her a hat, and she climbed into the passenger side of the pickup as two more men got in the backseat. "We're meeting the other men at the pasture gate." The ride was slow over the dirt road and across Slater land as snow flurries blew, and she looked up at the dull gray sky with concern.

They finally made it to the gate and saw the other trucks. One stood out. Garrett's pickup. Of course he would be here to help a neighbor.

She could deal with him for the sake of the cattle. The men unloaded the already-saddled horses. Josie went to Blondie and waited for Vance to give out the orders.

"It's a precaution, but I don't want anyone riding by themselves," he said. "We'll work in teams. When visibility gets bad, we quit and go back to the house."

Everyone climbed on their mounts and Garrett headed toward her. "Looks like we're a team."

Garrett knew that Josie wasn't happy, but he didn't care. He wanted to finish this and get back to his house and Brody. He was thankful he'd moved his herd yesterday.

"We'll take it slow," he told her as he directed his roan, Pirate, through the gate behind her. At first, she looked a little awkward on her horse, but soon found her stride.

"I can keep up with you," she told him.

She proved she was a woman of her word as she quickly rode behind the herd and managed to do her part.

It was slow going over the next few hours as the mamas and calves resisted going along with the move and kept trying to run off, but the worst part was the size of the snowflakes, and the snow was sticking, even with the wind.

Garrett kept thinking about a warm fire, some hot coffee and… He glanced at Josie. Why couldn't he stop thinking about her? He spotted a stray calf and got him back to the herd. He hated that she'd been distracting him ever since she'd showed up in Montana.

He pulled his scarf over his nose as the cold burned his skin. He turned to Josie and called out to her, "You okay?"

She nodded. "Just cold."

When suddenly another calf shot off, Josie kicked into Blondie's sides and went after it. Garrett waited about five minutes, but Josie didn't return.

"Dammit." With a call to Vance to let him know where he was going, he tugged Pirate's reins and headed in the direction she'd gone.

It wasn't long before the visibility turned bad. Dammit, he knew this wasn't good. He knew where he was, but did Josie?

He cupped his hand around his mouth. "Josie!"

With his heart pounding, he waited for some answer, but heard the roar of the wind. "Josie."

Finally, he heard his phone and pulled it out of his pocket. "Josie?"

"Hey, I might be lost," she said.

"Can you see any landmarks?"

"I'm next to a big tree. I passed over the creek a ways back."

"Stay there, I'm coming for you. Listen for my voice."

He adjusted his direction and kept calling out to her. He walked his horse through the snow building on the ground. Worry took over, and he knew he had to find her fast.

After a few minutes he was about to call for Vance when he yelled out her name again. This time he got an answer.

"Keep talking," he told her, and he finally found her. She had roped a small calf. "What the hell?" He climbed down and reached for her. "Are you crazy?"

"I thought I was doing my job."

"Well, going after one small calf isn't worth losing your life, or mine." He glanced around, knowing they had to get out of the weather. "Come on, I know where we are." He helped her back on her horse, then he climbed back on Pirate and pulled out his compass again.

"Think you can make it about a quarter of a mile to find shelter?"

She nodded and wrapped the rope attached to her calf and followed Garrett. He took out his phone and let Vance know that he'd found Josie and they were headed for the homestead cabin.

Garrett prayed they were headed in the right direction. There wasn't much visibility left as the storm intensified, but finally he saw the black stovepipe peeking out of the cabin's roof.

He stopped in front of the porch and lifted

her down from the horse, and began to carry her inside.

"Hey, I can walk," she argued.

"This is easier," he told her as he opened the door to the dark cabin and sat her down in a chair.

"I'll be right back as soon as I take care of the animals."

Shivering, she nodded. "I'm okay."

Garrett went back out and got the horses in the lean-to along with the calf. They were out of the weather, so he got some feed from the bin and pumped some water into the trough. He hurried back inside and found Josie had lit the lantern on the table and was putting wood into the stove. "Here let me do that."

She relented and sat back down in the chair. "I'm never going to hear the end of this, am I?"

He kept working. "Probably not." Once the fire caught, he turned back to her and took hold of her hands. "How are your hands, fingers?"

"They're fine."

"What about your feet. Do you still feel them?"

"Yes, they're fine. And no, I don't feel sleepy. I'm feeling great." She pulled her hands away. "So you can quit playing doctor."

"I didn't realize I needed to play keeper."

"Hey, that could have happened to anyone. The storm decided at that moment to get worse."

Just then, Garrett's cell phone rang. "Hey, Vance. Yes, we made it to the cabin."

"Then stay put," the foreman told him. "We barely made it back to the truck with the men."

"How'd the herd survive?" Garrett asked, knowing Josie wasn't going to be happy.

"They're safe as possible in these conditions."

"Well, count one more calf because we have him up here with us."

That got a laugh. "Stay warm. We'll come dig you out tomorrow."

Garrett hung up the phone and looked at Josie.

"So are they coming to get us?"

He shook his head. "Not until morning if the storm stops."

"What do you mean, tomorrow?"

"Josie, you were out in it. You saw that the visibility was close to zero. Do you really want to risk someone's life to come and get you because you can't stand to be anywhere near me?"

The small room was finally getting warm, but Josie was still miserable. Not because of the cold, but for the trouble she'd caused Vance and the men. She shouldn't have been so set on going after the calf.

"I'm sorry. I had no idea the storm was so bad, or how far the calf led me."

"Not a problem. I found you. Besides, this is a freak storm." The wind roared. "We have enough wood to keep us warm until someone comes for us."

That wasn't Josie's biggest problem. They were going to spend the night here. Together.

She sighed and looked around the rustic cabin that her great-grandparents built when George Slater brought his bride, Sarah Colton, here from Wyoming. There was the double bed against the wall with a nice quilt covering it. There was a small table and two chairs and a lantern in the center, also some personal items, candles, dishes and an assortment of canned food on the shelves. She had no doubt that someone had taken advantage of the cabin as their personal retreat. Ana and Vance?

Josie got up, went to the one window over the sink in the cabin and pulled back the curtains. A little more light came into the space. But there was nothing to see but blowing snow. She glanced across the room to find Garrett watching her.

"It's a good thing that Ana and Vance have made this place livable."

She folded her arms and nodded. "It doesn't

look too bad. And there's some food. Some canned stew and soup."

"And coffee," Garrett added. "But sorry, no inside facilities."

His words nearly made her laugh except she could really use a bathroom right now. "How far away is it?"

He did smile, and her heart took a little tumble. "Just a few feet around back behind the lean-to." He buttoned his sheepskin-lined coat and waited for her to do the same.

Once bundled up, he said, "Earlier, I strung a rope from the porch railing to the lean-to. We'll string another line to the outhouse."

Suddenly the seriousness of the storm hit her. She paused. "You can't see that far?"

"I'm not taking any chances if the storm gets worse. Call it a safety net."

She gave him a nod, and he opened the door to a gust of wind. Once outside, he took her by the arm and escorted her to the edge of the porch and the lead rope. Together they made their way to the lean-to. After checking the animals, they trudged on, fighting the strong winds and biting temperature as they found the small structure. They finished their business quickly, then headed back to the cabin.

He opened the door, and she practically tumbled into the warm room. "Oh, man, it's crazy out there," she breathed, feeling the cold burning her lungs. "How much worse is it going to get?"

"I can't answer that. We're safe here, though. Vance knows where we are, and we have enough firewood and food to keep us for a few days."

She went to the stove to warm up. "A few days? We're going to be here that long?"

Garrett pulled off his gloves and put his hat on the table, but left the hood to his thermal up. He was chilled to the bone. He walked to the heat.

"I can't say, Josie. This is a big storm front moving through. It's the reason we were moving the herd. And since we don't have a radio, I'm not wasting the charge on my phone to find out." He stood next to her. "In fact, you should shut off your phone, too."

She took it from her coat pocket. Her hands were shaking, so he took it from her and pressed the button. "Thanks."

He saw the fear in her eyes. "It's going to be okay, Josie. I'm just glad I found you."

She didn't look convinced. "If I hadn't taken off on my own, you'd be safely home in a warm bed."

"We can't change that. Besides, there's a bed here, and we'll be warm."

In the shadows of the fire, he could see her eyes narrow. "You're crazy, Temple, if you think I'm sharing a bed with you."

He knew ten years ago she'd have been eager to steal time away with him. He shook off the memory. "Why don't we find something to eat?" He went to the group of shelves and found a large can of stew. He also found some bowls and flatware. "Looks like Vance and Ana have all the conveniences of home."

Josie glanced around. "I recognize her touches."

"The old homestead looks good."

He worked the can opener. "They're going to build a house not far from here."

"Let me guess—you're going to build it for them."

He smiled. "We're working on some of the details. But not until the lodge is finished, and revenue starts coming in, then they'll break ground. I'd say late spring."

"That will be nice." Josie glanced at her watch. Two o'clock. It seemed later. She went to the window and looked out, but there wasn't anything to see through the blowing snow.

"Are you returning for their wedding?" he asked.

"Of course. Ana's my sister."

He dumped the contents of the stew in the pan, then took it to the cast-iron stove and placed it on top. "It shouldn't take too long."

He wasn't sure if that was a true statement.

Being alone with Josie Slater wasn't a good idea, not the way she still made him feel.

He released a long sigh. It was going to be a long night.

Later, with a mug of coffee in hand, and only the sounds of the wind and the crackling fire, Josie was still uncomfortable. She knew that she had to start up a conversation just to save her sanity.

"How long ago did your wife die?" Wonderful. Why not get personal, she thought.

He turned from the stove, where he'd just added wood. He walked to the shelves, looked inside and pulled out a bottle of wine. "Natalie died six months ago in a car accident, but she hadn't been my wife for two years."

"I'm sorry. I'm sorry that Brody lost his mother."

He went through the silverware bin and took out a corkscrew. "It's been tough on him, especially with our move here," he said. "Brody had been living with Natalie's parents since the divorce, so when I wanted to bring him here, I got a lot of resistance."

"It's tough for them to lose their daughter and now, their grandson moving away."

He opened the bottle and poured two glasses of wine. Setting them on the table, he returned to stir the stew. "It didn't help the situation when they tried to fight me for custody of my own son."

She felt a tugging on her heart as she retrieved some bowls and brought them to the table along with spoons. "I'm sorry, Garrett. I can see how much you love Brody."

He nodded and filled the bowls. He put the pan in the sink and came back to the table and sat down across from her. "Dig in."

She took a bite and realized she was really hungry. "This isn't bad." She took another bite.

He was eating, too. "Anything would taste good at this point." He sat back and took a sip of wine. "Now, this is good." He looked across the table at her. "What about you, Josie? Is there anyone special in your life?"

Whoa. She needed the wine now, and took a drink. "What is this? Secret confessions in a blizzard?"

"No, just curious how your life's going. We were a couple for a long time."

"Back when we were kids." She glanced away, then back at him. "What do you want me to say, Garrett? That there hasn't been anyone since you? Well, there have been, several, in fact."

Garrett didn't doubt that. Josie Slater was a beautiful woman. He could lie all he wanted, but truth was he'd never gotten over her. "You're too special to settle, Josie."

She glared at him. "Funny you'd be the one to tell me that. You didn't have any trouble walking away and finding someone else."

He leaned forward. "Your remembrance of that time seems to be a little different than mine. We broke up. Correction, you broke up with me."

"Because you weren't coming home for the summer," she argued. "We had plans."

"And as I explained back then, I was offered an apprenticeship with a large construction company. It was too good an opportunity to turn down."

She took a drink from her glass. "You didn't even discuss it with me."

"I tried. You weren't willing to listen to anything I had to say."

"So you went off, found someone and slept with her."

He froze at her words, but he quickly recovered. "Let's get that story straight, too. You broke up with me in May, saying we were finished for good if I took the job. Those were your exact words. When I tried to call you, you refused to talk to me. I met Natalie in July."

He was right. "Then why did you call me in September and tell me you loved me?"

Garrett remembered that night. It had been the night Natalie had told him she was pregnant. He stood and walked to the window. "I was drunk."

He heard her intake of breath. "That makes me feel so much better."

Hours later, neither one of them were talking much. Garrett had gone out again to check the horses. He'd asked her if she needed the facilities again. She went, but only to break up the boredom.

Once they returned, Josie looked around for something to read, but there was nothing, not even a magazine. Why would her sister need reading material with Vance around? No, she didn't want to think about how the two were lovers.

She went to the cupboard, thinking she could open another bottle of wine, but that wouldn't help. She didn't need to add to her problems. Somehow she had to get through this night and keep away from Garrett. And not just tonight but at the site, too. Maybe she could handle all the business with the job foreman, Jerry. Then Garrett wouldn't have to put up with her, either.

Garrett finished adding wood to the stove and the room was nice and warm. He went to the bed and drew back the quilt and blanket. Then he sat down and started pulling off his boots.

"What are you doing?" she asked.

"I'm going to bed."

She stared at him. "But—"

"We're going to share, Josie. Sorry, but I'm not sleeping on the floor." He lay back against the pillow and pulled the blanket up over his large body. "Oh, this feels good," he said, patting the spot next to him. "Join me. I promise to behave."

She was either too tired, or too mellow from the wine, to care. She walked over and sat down on the other side. Pulling off her coat and boots, she slipped under the blankets. It did feel good.

Garrett sat up and pulled the quilt over them. "It's going to get a lot colder later."

Not from where she was. Garrett's body was throwing off some serious heat. She had to resist curling into him.

"I'm sorry, Josie," he whispered into the darkness. "I shouldn't have said those things to you. We were kids back then, and I didn't always think clearly about all my choices."

The cabin was dim. Only the lantern on the table shed any light. Maybe that was what made her brave. "We were both wrong," she admitted. "You needed that apprenticeship. I just didn't want you to leave me. But you did anyway," she whispered. "You found someone else."

He turned toward her, his eyes serious. "There was never anyone except you, Josie. But things didn't work out for us." He paused. "When I married Natalie, I wanted my son to have a family, and I did everything possible to make that happen."

She started to speak, but he stopped her.

"Right now, Brody is my life. My focus is on his future. Also my dad needs me."

"You're a good father, Garrett," she told him, wishing she could turn back the clock for them.

His gaze met hers. He was too close and too tempting. "I've made a lot of mistakes, Josie, but I can't with Brody."

This was hard. They were supposed to have children together. "Of course he's got to be your first concern."

He leaned closer; she could feel his breath against her cheek. "I lied to you earlier."

She swallowed hard. "About what?"

"I did remember calling you that night. I missed you so much back then." He inched closer. "I didn't realize how much until I saw you again." Then his head lowered to hers, capturing her mouth in a kiss, so tender, so sweet that Josie was afraid to move.

She'd dreamed about this for so long. Slowly, her arms went around his neck, and she parted her lips. Garrett slipped his tongue into her mouth, and she couldn't help but groan as her desire for the man took over. It had been so long, but the familiarity was still there.

He pulled her closer against his body, and

her need intensified. He released her, but rained kisses over her face. "Josie, you feel so good. This is such a bad idea, but I don't care." His mouth took hers again, and he showed her how much he wanted her.

She was gasping for a breath by the time he broke off the kiss again. "Garrett," she whispered against his mouth, wanting more and more.

He finally released her. "God, Josie. I'm sorry."

She tried to push away, but he held her close. "Gosh, woman, I'm not sorry I'm kissing you. I'm sorry that I'm taking advantage."

"I'm a big girl, Garrett. I'll let you know if you're taking advantage."

He grinned and she saw his straight white teeth. "Maybe the best idea is to try and get some sleep." He turned her on her side and spooned her backside. "But we need to share body heat."

She didn't care what kept them close. She just loved the feeling and sharing the intimacy with this man. Maybe she wasn't truly over him.

CHAPTER SIX

JOSIE FELT A strong body pressing into hers, co-cooning her in warmth. It felt so good. She was too comfortable, too relaxed to move, and she snuggled in deeper.

That was when she heard voices. "I really hate to wake them. They look so…cozy."

Recognizing the man's voice, Josie struggled to open her eyes and blinked at the two figures. Finally, she managed to focus on Ana and Vance standing next to the bed.

Bed? "Oh, Ana. Vance."

She tried to sit up and quickly realized that she was pinned down by a strong arm. She glanced over her shoulder to find Garrett. Oh, God, a stream of memories flooded back. The snowstorm, the wine, Garrett's kiss… She felt the blush rise to her cheeks. Okay, this didn't look good.

"Garrett, wake up." She fought to separate them. "We've been rescued."

He refused to let her go. "Too cold to get up." He tightened his grip and snuggled against her.

Vance grinned. "We can come back if you need more time."

Ana swatted at her husband-to-be. "Stop it." She looked back at her sister. "Josie, are you okay?"

Josie managed to untangle herself from Garrett and sat up. "Yes, even better since you're here." She looked around and saw the sunlight coming through the window. "What time is it?"

"It's about eleven."

"Eleven in the morning?"

Her sister nodded. "The storm finally died out about 5:00 a.m. I was so worried about you two, I convinced Vance we should come and look for you." Ana eyed Garrett. "I'm just glad you found shelter when you got caught in the storm yesterday."

"It's a good thing we fixed up this place so you could enjoy the amenities," Vance said as Garrett finally sat up. "Hey, buddy, I see you survived." He glanced at Josie. "I'd say you two must have called a truce."

Josie practically jumped out of the bed. "We were only trying to keep warm." She tried not to make eye contact with Garrett, but she lost the battle. He, too, was remembering what had happened during the storm. "Unless you wanted us to freeze to death."

Garrett knew they'd been far from freezing last night. They'd gotten pretty heated up. "I had to wrestle her down to get her to cooperate. And her claws are sharp."

Ana went to the table and held up the empty wine bottle. "Looks like you had some help."

Garrett grinned and caught Josie's blush. "We ate in candlelight so…why not some wine?"

Ana started to reply when Vance said, "We better get you all back to the ranch. There's more snow coming."

Garrett pulled on his coat and followed Vance out to give the women a chance to straighten up the cabin while they got the horses ready. On the porch Garrett was greeted with a beautiful winter wonderland scene.

"This is quite a view." He nodded toward the mountains. "It's no wonder you want to build your house here."

Vance glanced at his friend. "There's not a prettier piece of land. So you better come up with a house design to do it justice."

Garrett placed his hat on his head. He'd already had some ideas. "I'll do my best."

They trudged through the snow to the lean-to and found the horses along with the calf had survived the storm just fine.

"So this is the little guy who caused all the trouble?" Vance asked as he knelt down to see the baby red Angus and looked for an ear tag or brand. "He must have been dropped late and missed the last roundup." The calf bawled in answer. "Okay, guy, we'll get you back home and get you something to eat."

They readied the horses, and Garrett led them to the front of the cabin as Ana and Josie came outside. Vance was carrying the calf.

Josie smiled, and Garrett felt the familiar stirring. "Oh, good, Storm's okay."

Vance looked at Josie. "Since when did you start naming livestock?"

She petted the calf. "He's had a rough time, and I doubt we'll find his mama."

"So does that mean you'll bottle-feed him?" Vance asked her.

Josie nodded. "I can."

"What about when you go back to California?"

Josie shrugged. "Maybe one of the ranch hands can take over."

Garrett swung up into the saddle and reached for the small animal as Vance lifted him up and helped lay the calf across Garrett's lap. He watched as Josie climbed on her horse, and for a second there he regretted having to return to reality instead of staying here with her. He wouldn't mind at all continuing those sweet, heated kisses and close out the rest of the world and make love all night.

Vance rode up beside him. "Something wrong?"

He shook his head. "No. Just thinking about what I need to do." First on the list was to stop thinking about Josie Slater. "I just want to get home."

"Then let's go."

They walked the horses through the deep snow for about a mile until they reached the road where a four-wheel-drive pickup with a horse trailer was waiting for them. Although the road had been plowed, it was still slow going back to the Lazy S especially with a bawling calf in the truck bed.

The backseat was tight, making Garrett very aware of the woman next to him. It was hard not to think about how her body was pressed against his all night. It had been a long while since he'd shared time or a bed with a woman. Not just any woman; someone who'd once been the love of his life. He'd quickly discovered there were still sparks between them.

They finally arrived back at the ranch, and Vance pulled up in front of the barn. When they got out of the truck, Garrett heard, "Dad! Dad!"

He turned toward the house and saw Brody

running down the steps and across the yard, struggling to get through the high snow.

Garrett hurried toward him and as soon as he got close enough, his son launched himself into his arms. "Dad, you're okay." Those small arms wrapped around his neck, and he caught his son's sob against his ear.

"Hey, Brody, I'm fine. Didn't Vance tell you that?"

The boy raised his head, wiped his eyes and nodded. "But the storm was so bad, and if you got really cold you could freeze to death."

Garrett swallowed back his emotions, seeing his son's fear of being left again. "Hey, I didn't. We were in a warm cabin that belonged to Ana and Josie's great-grandfather. We had a wood-burning stove and…" He started to say *bed,* but he saw his own father walking toward him. "And plenty of food."

"I'm glad. I thought you might never come home."

Garrett shook his head. "No, son, I was going to do everything to get back to you." He tried to lighten the mood. "It's you and me."

Brody smiled. "And Grandpa Nolan."

"And Grandpa Nolan," Garrett agreed, and set his son down on the plowed driveway as the man in question appeared and pulled him into a big hug.

"It's good you're safe," Nolan said.

"Yeah, it is." He searched his father's worried look. "Is everything okay? How did we fare at home?"

"Not too bad, but we lost electricity during the night, and service hasn't been restored yet, so there isn't any heat. Charlie and two of the hands took out some feed for the herd. They got a generator in the bunkhouse to keep them warm."

"We came here to wait for you," Brody said. "Mr. Colt invited us to stay here to stay warm. We sat in front of a big fire, ate popcorn and watched some movies."

Josie listened to the conversation, surprised that Colt would invite anyone into his house. She walked back to the truck bed while the ranch hands unloaded the horses from the trailer and took them into the barn for a well-deserved feed and brush down.

Vance got her calf down, and Brody came up to her and said, "Wow, is he yours?"

"I guess he is since he lost his mama. We'll have to feed him with a bottle."

Those so-like-his-father's green eyes lit up. "Can I help?"

Josie didn't want to do anything to keep Garrett here any longer, but how could she turn down this boy? "Sure, just check with your father."

She handed the calf's rope to Brody so she could greet the elder Temple. "Hello, Mr. Temple."

A big smile appeared on the man's weathered face. "Well, aren't you a sight for these old eyes." He grabbed her in a tight bear hug. "It's so good to see you, Josie."

"It's nice to see you again, too."

He released her. "It's about time you came back home. Although, I'm betting right now, you'd like some of the warm California weather."

"It would be nice right about now." She shivered. "But I have missed the snow, just not this much of it."

"And not getting lost in a blizzard." He sobered. "So glad that Garrett found you."

"Ah, I would have found my own way home eventually."

They laughed and heard someone calling to them. She looked up to the porch to see her dad waving at her.

"Come up to the house where it's warm."

She waved back. "Okay. As soon as we get the calf settled in."

Brody came up to them. "Dad, can I help Josie feed him?"

Ana spoke up. "I'm going to have to put my foot down. Everyone up to the house," she ordered, then turned to Vance. "Could Jake handle the calf until Josie gets something to eat and a warm shower?"

Okay, so she could use a shower. Josie realized she must look a mess. She turned to Brody. "It seems the boss has spoken. Maybe after we eat, I'll bring you down a little later."

The boy smiled. "Okay. I helped Kathleen make cookies and hot chocolate."

"Why didn't you say so earlier?" Josie smiled. "Come on." They headed to the porch where her father stood. "Dad, it's too cold for you out here."

"I can handle it." His blue eyes showed his concern. "I was w…worried about you." He reached for her hand and pulled her close and whispered, "I'm glad you're safe."

She closed her eyes and let the unfamiliar feeling wash over her. "I'm glad, too, Dad. I'm glad, too." She pulled back and smiled. "Now, I could use some coffee." She took his hand and together they walked into the house. It was good to be home.

An hour later, Josie was refreshed from a shower and feeling like a new person. Dressed in clean jeans and a sweater, she came downstairs to find Garrett and the rest of the Temple men sitting around the kitchen table with her father and Vance. She had no idea where Ana was.

She noticed that Garrett had on different clothes and looked like he'd showered and shaved. She couldn't help but think about last night. The feel of Garrett's body pressed against her, holding her during the long night.

"Josie." Brody spotted her first. He got up and came to her. "Are you going to go feed the calf now?"

"Brody," Garrett called as he stood. "Let Josie eat something first."

"I'm fine," she told him, then looked down at the boy. "How about we go in about an hour?" She had no doubt that the guests would still be here, so she might as well get used to it. "I'm sure Storm will be ready for another bottle by then."

Brody looked back at his father and got a nod. "Okay. Do you want something to eat? Kathleen left a plate in the refrigerator."

She didn't have an appetite right now. "I think coffee and maybe a few cookies would tide me over for a while."

Brody went to the cupboard and got her a mug and set it in front of the coffeemaker. "I can't pour it yet, not until I'm nine. My birthday isn't until May. May 19."

Josie didn't want to think about the child's conception, but she couldn't stop the addition. The boy was conceived sometime in August.

She poured her coffee, trying not to let her hand shake. She and Garrett had been broken up nearly three months.

She shook away the thought and took a sip. "Are you going to have a party?" she asked.

Brody shrugged. "I don't know. I don't have any friends here, 'cept Adam. He's in my class."

She could feel for the child. She always had her twin sister to be her best friend. "Well, you've only been in school a few days. And you still have six months to make more."

His eyes brightened and then he grinned at her. "Will you be my friend and come to my party?"

He was killing her. "I would love to be your friend, Brody. And thank you for the invitation, but I live in California. I don't know if I'm going to be here then."

Suddenly the smile disappeared. "Oh."

Great, she was breaking the boy's heart. "We'll see." She glanced at the table to see that she had an audience. Her gaze went from her father to Garrett. She wasn't going to answer any more questions from this group.

"Hey, Brody, I think feeding Storm might be a good idea."

"Now?" His eyes brightened once again.

With her nod, he went to his dad. "Dad, can I go and feed the calf?"

Garrett's gaze locked on Josie. "Sure. In fact, I'll go with you."

She didn't need this. She wanted to get away from the man. "Sure, the more the merrier." She walked off to get her coat.

Garrett got his son bundled up and put on his own jacket as Josie met them at the back door and they all left together.

Colt watched the threesome walk out together, then he turned back to Nolan. Over the years they hadn't exactly been friends. Of course, over the years, Colt Slater hadn't been friends with too many people.

Nolan and he had a falling-out years ago, but when Colt had called him to tell him about Garrett and learned about his lack of heat, he invited him to the house to wait out the storm. They'd managed to bury any bad feelings.

"Do you think there's any chance for them?" Nolan asked.

Colt picked up his mug and took a sip. "If the way they're looking at each other is any indication, I'd say yes. Only problem is, my daughter is pretty stubborn."

"As is Garrett," Nolan said. "He's been burned once." The man shrugged. "Of course, in my opinion he picked the wrong girl to start with. He's always belonged with Josie."

Colt nodded in agreement, but he also knew

that loving someone didn't mean you could keep them. He glanced at Nolan. He'd been happily married to Peggy for thirty years before she died from cancer a few years back.

Colt hadn't been as lucky to have that many years with Lucia. Only about a half dozen, and he'd thought they'd been happy ones, then she'd left him. Now he had his daughters—that was, if he could convince them to give him another chance.

He sighed. "Okay, what are we going to do to nudge them along?"

Nolan gave him a slow smile. "Well, I'd say this blizzard is helping the cause. I wonder if my son was smart enough to take advantage of last night." The man raised his hand. "Sorry, I didn't mean it like that."

"No offence taken. Josie has been an adult for a while, and I can't interfere in her business. But I heard from Vance that some wine was consumed and that they'd shared a bed—to keep warm of course."

Nolan shook his head. "And they think we're too old not to remember what it's like to be with someone you care about."

Colt remembered far too much. "So what do we do to help them?"

Out in the warm barn, Josie stood outside the corner stall as Garrett helped show Brody how to feed the calf.

"Keep the bottle tilted up," Garrett instructed the boy.

Brody giggled as he struggled to hold on to the bottle of formula. "He's wiggling too much."

"That's because he's hungry. You were like that, too. You couldn't get enough to eat."

"Did I drink a bottle like this?"

Garrett grinned. "Not this big, but yes, you drank from a bottle sometimes."

Josie had trouble thinking about Garrett sharing that experience with another woman. A woman who had his child, a child that she was supposed to have. *Stop it,* she told herself. That was another lifetime. She didn't get the guy or a child.

Brody looked at her. "You want a turn, Josie? It's fun."

"Sure." She took the bottle and immediately felt the strong tug. "Hey, this guy is a wrestler."

"Maybe you should rename him Hulk Hogan," Garrett said.

Josie couldn't help but laugh, recalling how Garrett used to watch wrestling on television. "Hey, Brody, did you know that your dad loves wrestling? He was a big Hulk Hogan fan."

The boy frowned. "Who's Hulk Hogan?"

She stared at Garrett. "You haven't taught your son the finer points of the WWF?"

"What's the WWF, Dad?"

Garret was shocked that Josie remembered that about the past. "The World Wrestling Federation. I'll tell you about it later." He leaned closer to Josie. "You enjoyed watching as much as I did."

She rolled those big blue eyes that had haunted him for years. "I was a teenage girl. I would enjoy just about anything my boyfriend liked."

She'd done that for him. She'd cared that much about him. It also surprised and saddened him that she'd pushed him out of her life. "So it wasn't Hogan's muscles?"

Josie's calf gave another long pull, this time throwing her off balance. He grabbed for her, but lost his balance, too, and all three went down in the fresh straw.

Brody began to giggle, then Garrett caught on and soon Josie joined the laughter. The white-faced calf cocked his head as if to say they were all crazy.

Garrett looked at Josie and mouthed a thank-you. He loved to see his son laugh as he tried to adjust to the move here. "Well, Brody, we better head for home." Garrett climbed to his feet and offered a hand to Josie and helped her up. "There's more snow coming."

The boy stood. "But our house is cold. We gotta keep Grandpa warm. You said it's not good for his arthritis."

"The electricity should be back on by now." Brody didn't look too happy as they walked out of the stall and went outside the barn to see more gray clouds and snow flurries in the air. His son ran ahead toward the house as Garrett walked beside Josie.

"Well, we've managed to survive the past twenty-four hours without killing each other." If he ever got a hand on her again, it definitely wouldn't be to harm her.

"Speak for yourself, Temple. I've had a few wayward thoughts."

He stopped. "I can't believe you remembered about Hulk Hogan."

She opened her mouth, and all he could think about was kissing her. Instead, he placed a gloved finger over it. "Too late to deny it."

"Okay, you got me." She blinked those incredible eyes at him. "Thank you again for finding me in the storm yesterday."

He shrugged. "Anytime, especially when we find accommodations as nice as the cabin." With a big bed, he added silently. "About those kisses…"

She froze, then quickly shook her head. "Hey, so we got a little nostalgic."

"Yeah, nostalgic," he mimicked, but all he could think about was capturing her lips once again. Bad idea.

Suddenly, they broke apart, hearing Brody calling to them. "Hey, Dad, guess what?"

"What, son?"

"Grandpa Nolan said we have to stay here tonight. The electricity still isn't fixed." A big grin appeared. "We're going to have so much fun."

Garrett looked at Josie. "Yeah. Fun."

CHAPTER SEVEN

THE DAY WAS a long one. Having to stay inside with the blizzard raging across the area made it worse. Everyone was uneasy as they stayed glued to the television news channel telling of the destruction.

Josie watched her dad and Vance either pace around, or call down to the barn to check on the men and the animals. Garrett held his cell phone to his ear, talking with his foreman at the Temple Ranch. She saw the concern on his creased brow.

This storm was deadly serious. Herds could be wiped out. That had been the reason they'd moved the cattle closer to the house so they could at least get feed to them.

She went to Garrett. "Is everything okay?"

He shrugged and put his phone back into his pocket. "We won't know until the storm is over. My men are okay, though. They have generators running in the bunkhouse and the barn. I don't know why the one for the house isn't working."

He nodded to Nolan. "I'm just glad Dad thought to bring Brody here."

Once again, she hated that she caused this problem. Garrett could have been home taking care of things if she hadn't gotten lost. "I'm sorry I caused all these problems for you."

He frowned. "You didn't cause the storm."

"But I was foolish enough to get lost. You would have been home dealing with your ranch."

He gave her that slow, sexy smile she remembered from so long ago. "And miss being with you last night?"

She gasped. "Stop making it sound improper. We didn't do anything."

He took a step closer. "You ever wonder what might have happened if Ana and Vance hadn't showed up? If we could finally have our night together?"

Only for the past eight years, she thought, then quickly shook off any memories. "Well, we're back here now, with family. There's plenty of room here, and because of Kathleen, we won't go hungry."

He looked at her, his eyes locked on hers. "Seems the elements are bent on throwing us together."

She glanced away. "It's a storm, Garrett, nothing more."

"Hey, Dad," Brody called.

Garrett started off, but stopped. "Maybe we should continue this discussion later."

She shook her head. "We can't look back, Garrett. Your son needs you."

He didn't move for a second or two, then he finally went to see what Brody wanted from him. She released a breath, glad he didn't push the issue. After last night, it would be easy to give in to her feelings. Wait. Wasn't that what got her hurt all those years ago?

The morning turned into a glum afternoon as the snow continued to fall. Josie tried to stay busy catching up with her work and went off to the den for some privacy.

About ten minutes later a young visitor showed up. Brody. The cute, inquisitive boy was polite and talked her into playing hooky. That was when she learned he was also a cutthroat video game player, beating her at everything.

"I give up," she cried. "You win."

The eight-year-old pumped his fist in the air. "I'll teach you to play better if you want." Those big green eyes sparkled in delight. "You can be good, too, Josie."

The boy was a charmer like his father. Watch out, all females, another Temple was coming soon. "And what happens when I get hooked on games and I spend all my days playing instead of working?"

Garrett stood outside the office door, listening to the conversation between his son and Josie. He was surprised at Brody. The boy hadn't been outgoing, especially with strangers, and it got worse since his mother's death. But something was happening between Brody and Josie.

Join the group, son. She's a real heartbreaker. He thought back all the years ago to that summer. He'd loved Josie, but he hated being so far away at college, and only getting to see her every few months. Getting married was the only solution, and that meant a job and working all summer to make enough money. When he'd gotten the apprenticeship with Kirkwood Construction it was so he could afford a wife and also get his college credits. Before he had a chance to propose marriage, Josie broke up with him.

Then that summer Garrett met Joe Kirkwood's daughter, Natalie. Four months later she was pregnant and they were married. He closed his eyes and thought how he should have worked harder on their marriage. He'd always regret that. Natalie might have wanted the divorce, but only because she knew that there was someone else who had his heart.

He closed his eyes. Did Josie still have his heart? He thought back to last night and how she felt in his arms. The familiar feelings…that he'd buried so far down that he didn't think they could ever surface, until last night when he'd held Josie again.

The sound of laughter brought him back to the present. His son's laughter. He pushed away from the wall and walked inside. He found Brody sitting across from Josie. They were playing some kind of card game.

Brody looked up. "Hey, Dad, Josie is teaching me to play War."

His gaze connected with Josie's. "Come on, Temple, join us. Unless you're afraid a girl will beat you."

Her eyes danced with mischief. He smiled. "That will be the day. Deal me in."

By afternoon, the daylight faded into darkness. Once again Garrett would be staying over, and although she hated to admit it, his presence made her restless.

She kept replaying their time together at the cabin. The kisses they'd shared. How his body felt against her. How secure she'd felt with him as the wind howled outside. She'd been far too eager to fall right back into Garrett Temple's arms. Storm or no storm, not a good idea.

She sighed and stole a glance across the room when Garrett got up from the sofa and walked through the wide doorway to the kitchen and the coffeemaker. After filling his mug, he leaned his hips against the counter and crossed his booted feet at the ankle then took a sip of coffee. Oh, yeah. The man was hard to resist.

Her gaze ate him up. He was tall with wide shoulders and a torso that narrowed to his waist and flat stomach. He was just long and lean. There wasn't anything about the man that she could complain about. And he still took her breath away.

Against her better judgment, Josie stood and walked into the kitchen. She told herself she wanted coffee, but mostly she wanted the man standing beside it.

"You don't have to spend your entire evening entertaining my son," he told her.

She poured a cup of coffee. "Brody's not a problem. You've done a fine job with him, Garrett."

"Thank you." His eyes met hers. "I wasn't always there for him like I should have been. I was busy building my business. I made money, but I think I lost the connection to my family." His sad gaze caught hers. "Sometimes you can't get that back. That's why Brody is so important to me. He deserves the best father I can be."

Unable to stop herself, she touched his arm. "I

can see how much you love him. And he loves you, too."

This time she saw the emotion in his eyes. "Sometimes we're lucky enough to get a second chance."

She didn't know how to answer that, but was grateful she didn't have to. A belly laugh escaped Brody as he rolled on the carpeted floor watching a cartoon video. She couldn't help but smile, too. Yet, she knew this child was a strong reminder of why she needed to keep her distance.

That little boy needed his father, and someone who could take over as a mother. That dream flew out the window a long time ago when the man she'd loved chose another woman over her.

Garrett's marriage to Natalie had broken her heart, and when she learned about the baby that nearly killed her. She shook away the sudden sadness. Another dream that had died was her hope of a life with Garrett. She turned to her career instead, and Slater Style had become her life. End of story.

After supper that evening, Josie decided to give up trying to work, but she still couldn't sit around, trying to avoid Garrett. So she went back to her Dad's office and found Ana there.

Her sister glanced up from the computer. "Hey, I'll be done in a few minutes."

Josie shook her head. "It's okay, take your time." With her tablet cradled in her arms, she sat down in the big leather chair across from the desk.

"Okay, I'm done," Ana announced, and turned away from the screen. "I emailed all the parents about tomorrow's school closures." She smiled. "Although, I think they can figure that out without me telling them."

"So you're staying home tomorrow?"

Ana raised an eyebrow. "I know you've lived in sunny California for a long time, but yeah, this storm will keep everyone indoors, but hopefully not for very long."

"Hope so, too," Josie said, not realizing she spoke out loud.

Her sister studied her. "Did you come in here because of our guests?"

Josie frowned. "Of course not. Besides, we can't send them home in this storm and without heat in their house."

Ana smiled and leaned back in her chair. "Of course there's always body heat. That seemed to work for you last night."

Don't blush, Josie told herself. It didn't work as she felt her cheeks heat up. "We didn't have much of a choice."

"I can't help but be curious about what happened between you two last night."

"Nothing," Josie denied and stood up. "I was stupid enough to get lost yesterday, and Garrett rode after me. He knew where the cabin was, thank God. We stayed there until you came by this morning. End of story."

Ana stood up, too. "Hey, I know you're having a rough time with Garrett being here, but I'm grateful he was there when you got lost. As for the rest of what happened at the cabin, it's none of my business," her sister said, then grinned. "And if sharing a bottle of wine helped make the night more bearable, more power to you."

There was no way she was ready to admit anything to Ana, nor did she want to analyze what happened between her and Garrett.

Time to get off this subject. "Since you'll be home tomorrow, maybe we can look at wedding dresses on the internet. It's only about six weeks until the big day."

Ana got all dreamy-eyed. "We're not planning anything too elaborate with the financial problems and all." She smiled. "Besides, I already found this incredible dress. It's at a consignment shop in Dillon. It's slim fitted and done all in creamy satin, covered with antique lace. The owner, Carrie Norcott, promised to hold it for me a few weeks."

A consignment shop? "This is your big day, Ana. It's my job to make it special, and on a budget. We can afford to get you a new dress."

"I know. Vance said the same thing, but wait until you see this one. It came out of an estate sale from Billings. It looks like something out of the 1930s and it's perfect for me. Besides, we don't have time to order a new dress and get it here in time."

Josie knew she wouldn't win this. "If it's what you want then that's one more thing off our list. Since we have the location locked down, the rest will be aisle runners, seating and decor."

Ana frowned. "Now with this early storm, I'm worried that the lodge won't be finished in time."

Josie hoped that Garrett wouldn't let them down, either. "All we need completed is the main room, one bathroom and the kitchen. We can do that. And as for decorations, it will be Christmastime. How do you feel about a Winter Wonderland theme? We place several pine trees on either side of the big picture window and add some poinsettias for color. An archway where that good-looking guy of yours can stand in his Western-cut tux. He'll have a perfect view of his bride coming down the aisle."

"Oh, Josie, it's perfect." Ana's eyes filled as she nodded, then pulled her sister into a big

FREE Merchandise is 'in the Cards' for you!

Dear Reader,

We're giving away FREE MERCHANDISE!

Seriously, we'd like to reward you for reading this novel by giving you **FREE MERCHANDISE** worth over $20. And no purchase is necessary!

You see the Jack of Hearts sticker above? Paste that sticker in the box on the Free Merchandise Voucher inside. Return the Voucher promptly...and we'll send you valuable Free Merchandise!

Thanks again for reading one of our novels—and enjoy your Free Merchandise with our compliments!

Pam Powers

Pam Powers

P.S. Look inside to see what Free Merchandise is **"in the cards"** for you!

HRLP-FM-09/13

W e'd like to send you two free books
to introduce you to the Harlequin® Romance Larger-Print series. These books are worth over $10, but they are yours to keep absolutely FREE! We'll even send you 2 wonderful surprise gifts. You can't lose!

REMEMBER: Your Free Merchandise, consisting of **2 Free Books** and **2 Free Gifts**, is worth over $20.00! No purchase is necessary, so please send for your Free Merchandise today.

Plus TWO FREE GIFTS!
We'll also send you two wonderful FREE GIFTS (worth about $10), in addition to your 2 Free Harlequin Romance Larger-Print books!

Visit us at:
www.ReaderService.com

hug. "Thank you for coming home. You'll never know how much it means to me."

Josie pulled away, fighting her own tears. "I wouldn't miss it for anything."

Ana grew serious. "Then would you consider being my maid of honor?"

Josie felt tears welling in her eyes. "Oh, Ana. I'd love to." She hugged her sister.

Josie pulled back, wiping away tears, when she saw Vance and Garrett; both were bundled up in their coats. It was obvious they'd been outside.

"Oh, Vance. Josie was talking about the wedding. She's going to be my maid of honor." She went to her future husband. "And it's going to be a Christmas theme."

He kissed her. "Just tell me it's going to be this Christmas and I'm a happy man."

Ana laughed, and Josie turned her attention to Garrett. Once their eyes locked, she felt the pull. She couldn't help but think about being stranded in the cabin with the man's arms wrapped around her.

Josie heard her name. "What?"

"I wondered if you'd like some hot chocolate?" her sister asked.

"Sure, but I need to get some work done."

"I'll bring it to you here." She started out and stopped. "Oh, and Vance asked Garrett to be his best man." The couple walked out, but Garrett stayed.

Great. The last thing she wanted or needed was more time with this man. "Do you need something?"

"You don't want to talk about our duties as maid of honor and best man?"

She glared at him.

"Okay, how about we talk about the lodge. I was thinking when this weather clears we should get back to work on it. If the electrical is roughed in, then we can get the heat on and begin to drywall the inside."

She frowned. "I thought when the electrical was finished, your job was done and we take over."

Garrett shrugged. "I don't mind helping out so the wedding will come off on schedule. I'd hate to have them move the ceremony to the courthouse."

Josie shook her head. "I won't let that happen, but there isn't much extra money right now for the work."

Garrett walked toward her, and she had to fight to stand her ground. "I didn't say I would charge. I'll be doing the work myself, not my men."

"You?"

"Hey, I can still hang Sheetrock, even tape

and mud the seams. And my carpenter skills are pretty good, too." She watched his delicious mouth twitch at the corners. "I still have a tool belt."

Oh, God. She didn't need to picture Garrett in a tool belt. "What about the time? Surely you have other jobs to do."

"With this weather there isn't much work right now, just a few small residential jobs that Jerry can handle. What do you say, Josie? You want to be my helper?"

No! She didn't need to spend any more time with this man, but the sooner the job got done the better. First the wedding, then the lodge could open for paying customers. Then she could go back to California and forget all about Garrett Temple. "Apprentice. I like that title better."

About midnight, Colt sat by the fire in the family room and watched the flames dance, holding a glass of whiskey in his hand. He was probably breaking all the rules drinking alcohol, but right now he didn't give a damn. Sometimes a man needed a stiff drink. He was tired of his solitary bedroom and more dreams about Lucia.

The house was quiet even though there were three guests. Ana and Vance had gone off to the foreman's house across the compound to spend the night. They'd given up their bedroom upstairs to Garrett and Brody. Nolan had been assigned to his youngest daughter, Marissa's, bedroom. He smiled, hoping his neighbor liked pink.

Josie had gone upstairs to her room hours ago. He had no doubt that had been to keep the distance between her and Garrett. The two had spent most of the day trying to stay out of each other's way. But there were sparks flying everywhere.

"Mind if I join you?"

Colt looked up and saw Nolan standing in the doorway. He still wore his jeans and the shirt he had on earlier, but the boots had been replaced with a pair of moccasins.

"Not at all. Come in and pour yourself a drink."

That got a smile from the sixtysomething neighbor. "Don't mind if I do." Nolan walked to the bar, took down a glass from the shelf and poured a splash of bourbon. He made his way to the other overstuffed chair across from Colt.

Nolan's dark gaze met his. "Couldn't sleep?" he asked.

"Seems that's all I do these days," Colt murmured. "I hate it." He smacked the cane beside his chair. "Can't wait until I lose this, too."

"Hey, you might be losing one, but I'll probably be taking up one soon with this dang arthritis." He ran a hand over his thinning gray hair. "But I can't say I'm unhappy that my son and grandson moved back home. He's doing a great job of running the operation." He smiled. "I have to say that my grandson really lights up that old house."

Colt knew his neighbor had been lonely since his wife, Peggy, died. Colt was ashamed he hadn't stayed in touch with his neighbor. "I love having Ana back, and now Josie's home." But soon Ana would marry Vance and Josie would go back to L.A.

Nolan took a drink and nodded. "I've sure enjoyed spending time with that sweet Josie of yours. I've noticed that Garrett liked it, too." He sighed. "I wish I could have helped those two out years ago. Maybe if I'd stepped in, things would have turned out different."

Colt sighed. "Did any of us listen to common sense when we were young? We had all the answers. Maybe they'll find a way to get together this time around."

Nolan nodded. "Got any more ideas?"

"Well, since this storm is expected to move out tomorrow, you can't use that excuse any longer to stay here."

"We might not have to," Nolan said. "Garrett told me that Josie is going to work with him on the lodge."

"Well, dang. That's not going to help much with the crew around."

Nolan shook his head. "No, the men won't be there. They have another job. They both decided this was going to be a wedding gift for Vance and Ana. They want to make sure the lodge is finished in time for the wedding."

Colt nodded. "That's a lot of time together. If your boy doesn't take advantage, there's no hope."

Garrett lay on the bed until he heard Brody's soft snores. The kid had been hyped up most of the day. Of course, he'd gotten a lot of attention. He'd even let his son go out to bottle-feed the calf.

Garrett stood and slipped on his jeans and shirt, but didn't bother with the buttons. He grabbed his shaving kit that his dad had brought over to the Slaters earlier and went down the hall to the bathroom. He quickly went through his nightly routine. Once he'd brushed his teeth, he put everything back, but left the small leather bag on the counter next to Josie's things.

He paused a moment to inhale the scent of her shampoo and soap that were so her. He wasn't going to get much sleep tonight. He stepped out into the hall and nearly ran into a petite body— Josie. He reached for her as she gasped.

"Sorry, I didn't know anyone was in here," she whispered.

"I just finished up." He watched as her tongue began to lick her lips. The memories of last night flooded his head. Josie in his arms, his mouth covering hers, hearing her soft moans.

"It's all yours," he finally managed to say, but he didn't move. He glanced down at her flannel pajamas and thought how sexy she looked.

As if she could read his mind, she said, "They keep me warm."

"Last night, I kept you warm."

She frowned, but he saw the blush. "That was an emergency."

"So is this." He gripped her arms and walked her backward into her bedroom, then his mouth covered hers.

It was heaven. Oh, God, he couldn't get enough of her as he drew her close, loving the feeling of her lush body sinking into his. Last night he'd been a fool to turn her away. He broke off the kiss, only to trail kisses down her jaw.

"Garrett…"

He pulled back, hearing her plea, but desire overtook him. His mouth returned to hers; he angled her face and deepened the kiss.

"I'd wanted to do this all day," he breathed against her lips in between teasing nibbles.

Then reality quickly intervened with the

sound of someone out in the hall. He broke off the kiss and pulled her close.

They waited in the dark bedroom until the bathroom door opened and closed. He looked down at her, still feeling her heavy breathing. Then she pulled away and hugged herself. He suddenly realized what might have happened if they hadn't been interrupted. Not wise.

This wasn't the time to continue this. "I should get back to my room. Good night, Josie."

He left her, knowing there wasn't any future in starting up something with Josie or any woman right now, especially a woman who had a home and career in California. Over a thousand miles away.

So now he had to figure a way to keep his distance for another few weeks. He should be able to do that. So why had he asked her to work with him? Was he crazy? He groaned. Yeah, he was crazy about Josie Slater.

It took two days for the ranch to get back to operating as usual. The storm had taken its toll with downed fences and lost cattle. Not too bad, considering the intensity of the blizzard's destruction, Josie thought as she pulled up to the construction site.

She'd spent the past forty-eight hours trying not to second-guess her decision to help Garrett with the inside of the lodge. She thought back to the other night and the breathtaking, toe-curling kiss. What frightened her more was what might have happened if Brody hadn't gotten up. Would things have gone further than just a kiss? No! She couldn't let the man back into her life. There was no future with Garrett Temple.

Josie parked Colt's four-wheel-drive pickup next to Garrett's truck. She stepped out onto the still-frozen ground, wrapped her scarf around her neck and made her way down the plowed path to the lodge. She smiled at the two-story rough-log structure with the green metal roof. The chimney stacks were covered in river rock and the wraparound porch also had rough-log railings, adding to the rustic look.

"You do good work, Garrett Temple."

She walked up the steps to the double doors with the cut-glass insert that read River's End Lodge. That one extravagance was well worth it. She ran her fingers over the etched letters.

She felt her excitement build as she opened the door and stepped inside. It was hard to take it all in. So many things drew her attention as she glanced around the nearly finished main room. The dark-stain hammered hardwood floors, partly covered for protection in the traffic areas were well-done. She moved on to the huge river rock fireplace. The raised hearth had room for a dozen people to sit down and warm themselves.

She walked past the staircase, arching up toward the second-floor landing, a wrought-iron railing with the Lazy S brand symbol twisted in the design. Okay, another splurge. Her gaze continued to move around the room, seeing special touches that made this place more cozy and comfortable. It could almost be someone's home. At the wall of windows, she looked at the river and the mountain range. Amazing view. Okay, she was definitely going to push this place for weddings.

She heard a noise upstairs, then a loud curse. Garrett. Hurrying to the steps, she made her way to the second floor and went on to search room to room. She started to call out his name when she spotted him and froze.

His back was to her and what a sight. A tool belt was strapped low on his waist and he wore faded jeans that hugged his slim hips and long legs. Her gaze moved to his dark T-shirt emphasizing his wide shoulders and muscular arms.

He was balancing a sheet of wallboard and trying to reach for a tool. Then he glanced at her. "Well, are you going to stand there or help me? Hand me that screw gun."

Josie shot across the large bedroom and reached for the electrical tool he'd pointed at.

Once he had it in his hand, he said, "Here, hold this up." He nodded to the large sheet of wallboard. Once she pressed against it, he began to work on adding screws into the edges. "There, that does it." He looked at her. "So you finally decided to come to work."

"You said I could come when I had time. I need to check in with my office, and there's a few hours' difference between here and Los Angeles. If you wanted me here at 7:00 a.m., you should have told me."

Garrett hated that he'd snapped at Josie. He'd almost called her and told her not to come at all. After the other night and that kiss, he didn't need to spend any more time with her. He should have gotten one of his men. No matter what it cost.

"Sorry. I'm an early riser and just take it for granted everyone else is."

"I am, too. But I'm trying to run my business long-distance. There's a big wedding I'm coordinating a few weeks from now. My assistant is doing a great job, but she still has to run everything by me."

He walked over to the drywall compound and seam tape. "Sounds like your business is doing very well."

She shrugged. "I do well enough, but long-distance is hard, especially since I'm not able to do bids on jobs."

He nodded, loving the look of her in her jeans and sweatshirt. He liked her better in her pj's. *Don't go there,* he warned. "Okay, you ready to go to work?"

"Sure, what can I do?"

He handed her a long, narrow pan partly filled with a white compound and a putty knife. "We need to fill all these screw holes."

She glanced around the room. He knew that she was silently counting the thousands of screw heads. "Okay. I'm not sure how good I'll be."

"You'll be great."

He gave her a quick lesson, put her in front of one wall, and he went to the other end.

It wasn't long before they met in the middle. He was surprised at the progress they'd made. But it was only one room.

"Garrett," she began. "Not to complain, but how many rooms do we have to do?"

"Actually, all the rooms have been drywalled."

She turned to him, and he could see spots of compound on her cheek. "Wait, I thought you said that wasn't in our contract with GT Construction."

He shrugged. "It wasn't that much more in cost. Besides it was going to be a lot more work for us. It was easier to have one of my men do the hanging."

"Then I want to pay for half," she argued.

"Josie, that's not necessary."

She glared at him. "You can't take all the cost. I want to pay, too."

"Why are you being so stubborn about this?"

Her eyes widened. "Because you asked me to help with this project and we agreed to work together." She paused. "If I were a man, you'd gladly take my money."

"If you were a man, I wouldn't be thinking what I'm thinking right now."

Josie worked hard to keep her composure. She couldn't let Garrett know how his words affected her, but she didn't want to deal with this all the time. She put down her mudding pan, grabbed her coat off the sawhorse and headed for the door. She never got there because Garrett grabbed her by the arm and turned her around.

"You want me to apologize for kissing you the other night? Why, Josie? You didn't stop me then." His gaze was heated. "Are you going to stop me now?" He leaned toward her and his mouth closed over hers.

Josie was ready to push him away, but the second his lips touched hers everything changed. She moaned and her arms wrapped around his neck, holding him there, afraid he would stop. Then he drew her against him, and she could feel his desire, his need for her.

He broke off the kiss. "God, Josie... What you do to me. What you've always done to me."

She hated how he made her feel vulnerable again. "I guess this isn't getting much work done. Besides, your tool belt is digging into me."

Grinning, he released her. "I can take it off."

Keep it light. "Thanks for the offer, but we need to get to work. We have a wedding in a month."

She caught his look, but ignored the pain she'd felt remembering their own wedding plans so long ago. She'd learned the hard way they were foolish dreams.

CHAPTER EIGHT

OVER THE NEXT five days Josie worked long, hard hours at the lodge with Garrett, then spent evenings with Ana, Vance and her father. Exhausted, she slept very well at night. She valued those hours of slumber, but it didn't look like she was going to get many tonight.

It was her duty as maid of honor to do a bachelorette party for the bride. So on Friday afternoon, the celebration began. She'd gone with Ana to see her sister's wedding dress in Dillon. Josie fell in love with the gown and agreed it was the perfect choice.

Once finished with shopping they stayed in town, and the plan was to meet some of Ana's friends for dinner. The three women—Sara Clarkson, a longtime friend; Clare Stewart, another school friend; and Josie—all convinced Ana to go into the Open Range Bar and Grill.

If they were going to misbehave tonight they wanted it to be away from their small community. The surprise was they were headed off to a honky-tonk for a few drinks to celebrate the upcoming wedding. Josie hadn't expected her commonsense older sister, Analeigh, to be so eager to go.

Inside the bar, Josie looked around the rustic-looking room that was a little raunchier than she liked. Although, it didn't seem to bother anyone else but her. It was crowded with people, and a country-Western song was blaring from the DJ booth. The dance floor was filled with couples two-stepping to the latest Tim McGraw song. This wasn't Josie's kind of fun, but seeing the look on Ana's face was priceless.

Her sister leaned toward her and cupped her mouth. "I've heard about this bar—I can't believe I'm really here."

"Every girl needs a send-off," Josie said, and glanced at the bartender, Tony. She'd spoken to him earlier, and he'd been happy to help out. "Come on, let's go find a table."

She took her sister's hand and pulled her through the crowd until she spotted a table that had a sign on the top. Reserved for Slater Sisters.

"Oh, look." Ana sighed. "Did you do this?" she asked Josie.

Josie smiled. "A phone call," she yelled over the music.

They sat down just as the music ended, and Clare said, "Oh, my, look at all the guys."

"I'm not looking. I've already found mine," Ana said.

"You are so lucky to have Vance, Ana," her friend Sara told her.

Her sister got that dreamy look again. "I know. And he's been right under my nose for years."

Josie recalled the runaway boy, Vance Rivers, that their father had taken in. Of course, back then she and her sister were jealous because Colt had paid more attention to Vance than his own daughters. Josie realized now that it wasn't Vance's fault.

The young waitress dressed in a little T-shirt, a pair of jeans and boots took their drink order, margaritas all around.

Clare drew their attention. "You know who else is a really good-looking man? Garrett Temple." The blonde looked at Josie. "Do you still lay claim on the man, or do the rest of us get a chance with him?"

Josie stiffened as all eyes turned to her. She found she wanted to ward them off, but she hadn't the right to. "It's been years since Garrett and I were a couple. Besides, I'm headed back to L.A. soon."

The music started up again, and the waitress brought over their drinks. Josie handed over her credit card for the first round as Sara and Clare got up to go to the dance floor with two guys.

Ana leaned over and said, "Sorry, I don't want Clare to bring up bad memories."

Josie shook her head and took a drink and tasted the salt along the rim. "It's okay, Ana. Everyone here remembers Garrett and I together. I can handle that."

"Good." They drank and caught up on local news the past years. Soon the music turned to a fast-paced song, and everyone got up to do a popular line dance. Ana grabbed Josie's hand. "Come on, I want to dance."

Lined up on the floor next to Ana, Josie began to do the steps. She laughed as she messed up, but then finally caught on and got the rhythm. Maybe this night would be fun after all.

It was nearly eleven o'clock. This wasn't how Garrett wanted to spend his Friday evening as he walked into the Open Range Bar behind his friend Vance. He could smell sweat and liquor.

Vance had called him earlier and said his friend the bartender, Tony, had phoned him about a party with the Slater sisters and was worried about them driving home.

Garrett glanced around the crowded room and the couples dancing, or cuddled up together at tables. There were still guys lined up three deep at the bar looking hopeful they'd find that special girl, at least for tonight.

He'd never been the type to hang out in places like this. He'd been married and had a child when he was barely the legal age to drink alcohol.

"You sure they're still here?" He wasn't too upset that he'd get a chance to see Josie. Would she be happy to see him? Would she be with another guy? She'd been keeping her distance at the lodge, making sure she worked in another area.

"Yes. Tony called and he's been watching the party for the past few hours. It seems they've been drinking tequila shots. He wanted to make sure they got home safely. Thanks for helping out, friend. I wasn't sure if I could handle all four of them."

"Not a problem." Garrett was more worried that Josie would be angry that he came to break up the party.

Vance pointed toward the table. "Hey, there they are." He started in that direction, and Garrett followed him.

When the girls spotted him they cheered, and Ana jumped up and threw herself into her future husband's arms. "Vance, you came to my party."

He kissed her. "I hope you don't mind. Garrett

and I wanted to make sure you ladies got home all right. It's a long drive back."

"Oh, that's so sweet," Ana said. "But first you have to dance with me." She tugged Vance's hand, leading him onto the floor. Soon Ana was plastered against her man.

Garrett couldn't help but look around for Josie. He soon discovered her on the dance floor with some guy. He stiffened, seeing the man's hand moving lower on her hip. He immediately walked through the crowd. "Excuse me, but would you mind letting go of my…girlfriend?"

The shorter man with the wide-rim Stetson glared back.

Garrett stole a glance at Josie, then back at the guy. "Look, we had a big fight and she left. I went out looking for her to tell her how sorry I was." His gaze locked on hers again. "I'm sorry, darlin'. Will you forgive me for being such a jerk?"

Josie opened her mouth to speak, but instead, Garrett reached for her and planted a kiss on her lips to convince her dance partner of his intentions. When he'd released her—not that he cared—the stranger had disappeared.

"I guess he's gone," he told her, but he couldn't get himself to release her. She felt too good in his arms.

"What are you doing here?" she asked.

The music started up again with the Miranda Lambert song, "Over You." Garrett pulled Josie close and began to move to the slow ballad. The feel of her body against him had him groan in frustration. "Dancing with you."

"No, really, what are you doing here?" she whispered against his ear.

He wondered the same thing himself. "The bartender is a friend of Vance's. So we came to drive you ladies home," he told her as he led her around the dance floor to a secluded corner.

"I can manage getting everyone home," she told him. "And I can handle groping men."

He pulled back and looked in her eyes. "I guess I didn't need to kiss you to get rid of the guy."

"No, you didn't need to do that," she answered weakly, but he saw the desire in those cobalt-blue depths.

"What a shame, that was my favorite part." He placed another sweet kiss against her lips.

She swallowed hard, wanting more. "Garrett…"

Before she could finish, Ana and Vance danced toward them, and Ana said, "Oh, Josie, I'm having so much fun. This is the best bachelorette party I've ever been to."

Vance frowned at Ana. "Since when have you been to any other ones?"

Ana giggled. "I haven't, but this is still the best because it's mine." She wrapped her arms around Vance's neck. "And you're going to be my husband. Oh, I love you so much." She planted a kiss on her groom.

Vance finally pulled back. "Hey, honey. Why don't I take you home?" He leaned in and whispered something in her ear that had her smiling.

Ana turned to Josie. "We're going home now." She wrapped her arms around her sister. "Thank you so much for the party. It was fun to spend time with you."

"You're very welcome," Josie said. "Don't worry, I'll make sure Clare and Sara get home."

She looked at Garrett. "You can go, too."

He shook his head. "Not on your life, darlin'. I'm you and your ladies' designated driver tonight. You got a problem with that?"

God help her. Josie shook her head and handed him her keys. "Not a single one."

The next morning, Josie slept in later than usual, but felt she'd earned the extra hour. After all, it was Saturday. She went down to the kitchen and had a quiet breakfast while Colt joined her with coffee, but there wasn't any sign of Ana or Vance.

She thought about Garrett and last night. He'd insisted that he drive her car, and then made sure that Sara and Clare had gotten home. During the ride back to the ranch, Josie realized she'd had more to drink than was safe to drive. Although she wouldn't admit it to Garrett, she liked that he'd taken care of her. She just couldn't let herself get too used to having him around, not when their futures were headed in different directions.

She only had to hold on a few more weeks. She needed to make it through Thanksgiving, then soon came the wedding.

Refilling her mug, she headed to the office to work. She knew the safe way to avoid temptation was to avoid Garrett altogether. She might just have a solution to the problem.

Josie walked in, sat down at the desk and dialed Tori for an update on upcoming events.

"Slater Style," her twin answered.

"So we're still in business?"

Tori groaned. "It's crazy here. Do know how many parties are scheduled for the holidays?"

Josie smiled. "Yes, I've been following the bookings Megan sent me, and we've gone over things."

153

Megan Buckner had been her assistant for over two years. The woman had really stepped up and taken over two jobs. Of course, Josie hadn't planned on being gone from L.A. this long.

"We need more help," Tori said. "I'm not sure I can do these parties myself."

Josie knew she'd put a lot on her sister's shoulders, but she figured there was something else on her mind.

"Tori, Megan has the list of regular employees we hire for big parties. What's really wrong, sis? Did something happen?"

She heard the long sigh. "No, it's not the business. It's just…"

"What? Is it Dane? Is he bothering you?"

There was a long silence.

This wasn't like her twin. "Tori, tell me."

"I have no proof it's him, Josie. I know he's watching me, but as far as I know, he hasn't violated the restraining order. And yes, I called Detective Brandon like you suggested. He said the police's hands are tied, too."

Josie closed her eyes. "I'm sorry, Tori. I shouldn't have left you alone. I called to tell you that I'm getting the next flight to L.A. At least I can take some of the business pressure off you."

There was a pause, then Tori said, "It's great you're coming back, but I don't want you to get involved with my trouble. Dane will just get angrier."

Josie was frustrated. "Fine, but we need to handle this situation, Tori."

"I know. Please, can we talk about something

else? I'm worried about the wedding in Santa Barbara. Will you be here in time for that?"

Josie knew how important the Collins/Brimley wedding was to her. Both affluent families, they could bring her future business, or give her a bad name, and Slater Style would be finished. "Yes, I'll be there Friday."

Josie asked to speak with Megan. When her assistant came on the line, it wasn't long before Josie knew everything was under control, but the wedding party's families were concerned about Josie's absence. "Thanks for all your work, Megan. Will you put Tori back on the phone?"

"What do you need, sis?" Tori said.

Josie went over the flight time, then added, "I want you to be careful, Tori. Dane has already proved he can be violent. So don't go out alone at night and set the alarm in the house."

With Tori's promise, Josie said her goodbyes and hung up the phone. That was when she caught Garrett's large figure in the doorway. His sheepskin jacket was open, revealing a fitted Western-cut shirt and jeans over his slim hips and long legs. His cowboy hat in hand.

She ignored her racing pulse. "Garrett, is there something wrong?"

He held up her keys as he walked across the room, his gait slow and deliberate. He'd driven her car home last night, then used the vehicle to get himself back to his place. "And I stopped in to see how you were feeling this morning."

She shook her head, barely able to meet the man's gaze. "You don't have to babysit me." Then she quickly added, "I appreciate you taking me home last night. Thank you."

He smiled and it did things to her. "You're welcome," he told her, but didn't leave.

"Is there something else you need?"

"Just some input on the lodge. I have some countertop samples I need you to look at. Charlie's brought my truck, and the samples are inside."

"What happened with the ones we picked out two weeks ago?"

"They didn't have enough granite slabs to do the entire lodge."

"Okay." She glanced back at the computer screen. "Give me a few minutes. I need to book a flight to L.A. first."

He frowned. "You're leaving?"

She nodded. "Just for the weekend." She continued to scan through the flights. "I've been contracted to do a large wedding, and I need to be there."

Garrett already knew from the conversation it was more. "Is that the only reason?" He sat down on the edge of the large desk. "Is an ex-boyfriend bothering her?"

Josie hesitated, then nodded. "Dane hasn't broken any laws yet, but I'm worried about Tori's peace of mind. It's getting to her."

"My offer is still good. I can call my friend." Why did he keep getting mixed up in her life? "He's a private investigator and might be able to help."

"I appreciate your offer, Garrett, but when I go to L.A. I plan to bring Tori back here. She can work her web design business from here and help me with Ana's wedding." Her fingers worked the keyboard on the webpage.

Just leave, Garrett told himself. *She doesn't want your help.* "Book me a seat, too."

She jerked her head around to look at him. "You? You can't go."

He shrugged. "Why not? Someone's got to watch out for you two."

Her eyes widened. "For one thing, Tori and I have handled things on our own for a long time. Secondly, we're not your problem."

"I'm Vance's friend, and you're his family. Besides, there's a jerk out there who's making your sister's life miserable. What would Ana do if she knew?"

Josie shook her head. "She doesn't need this worry. I can take care of Tori."

His stomach tightened at the thought of some jerk possibly hurting her or her twin. "Josie, I can't just stand by and let someone hurt either you or your sister. What if I'm a deterrent for this guy? Wouldn't my presence help keep him away? Although I wouldn't mind taking a few jabs at him."

He watched her fight with his reasoning. "Okay, say it does, it still doesn't solve the problem."

"Let's just see the situation, then go from there."

"Wait, what about Brody? You can't leave him."

"Brody will be in Bozeman at his grandparents' house. It's a three-day weekend from school. So I'm all yours."

She didn't look convinced.

"This is your sister we're talking about, Josie. We wouldn't want to take any chances with her safety. We'll just tell Tori that I'm helping you with the event."

Those blue eyes bored into his. "This still isn't a good idea."

Hell, he already knew that, but it was too late to stop. He wanted to be with Josie.

Friday afternoon Josie found herself seated next to Garrett on an early-morning flight to Los Angeles. She'd been grateful he hadn't said much and she was able to get some work done. He'd slept.

When they'd landed at LAX, Garrett got a rental car, and knowing that Tori would be working at home, they drove straight to the town house that she shared with her twin.

Garrett pulled into her parking spot, but Josie hesitated before going inside. "I don't want you grilling Tori. She's been very secretive about her relationship with Dane, and when things turned abusive it made her more ashamed."

"It's not my place to tell her what to do. I only want to help her."

"She probably isn't going to want to share much of her personal life."

Garrett glanced away from the road. "Then you're going to let her think that you trust me, that we're friends again. More than friends."

She glared at him. "Garrett, I don't want to trick Tori into thinking anything like that."

He shook his head. "Look, Josie. This Dane guy seems like a loose cannon. He's already hit Tori, and now he seems to still be hanging around."

Josie knew what he said was true. This could be a dangerous game. "Okay, let's go inside and see how things are, but please don't mention anything about a private investigator."

He nodded. "Okay."

She didn't let go of his arm. "Have I told you how glad I am that you're here?"

He smiled. "You just did."

They got out of the car in an area off Los Feliz Ave. This was old Los Angeles, where some structures were built in the 1930s. Their home was once an apartment that had been converted into town houses.

The Spanish-style building had original tile and archways, and that had been what drew Josie to the place. And nearly a year ago, Tori moved in with her after her breakup with Dane. She could still see her sister's battered face after he'd used her for a punching bag.

Josie used her key in the door, then immediately called out to Tori.

"Hey, is anyone home?"

In a few seconds, a petite woman came down the hall. Vittoria had glossy black chin-length hair and midnight eyes. Her twin had inherited their mother's Hispanic skin tone.

"Josie!" She picked up speed and soon the sisters were locked into a big embrace. "I'm so glad you're here."

Josie pulled back. "Why? Has something else happened?"

Tori quickly shook her head. "No, I'm fine. I just missed you these last few weeks." Her gaze shifted to Garrett, and she frowned. "Well, I'm surprised to see you here. Hello, Garrett."

"Hello, Tori. It's good to see you again."

Tori didn't smile. "Do you have business in L.A.?"

He glanced at Josie. "No, I just came to help your sister." He put their suitcase down on the tiled floor. "I hear there's a big wedding in Santa Barbara."

Tori placed her hands on her hips. "Okay, someone tell me what's going on here."

Garrett wasn't sure how much he should say. So the truth might be a good start. "Okay, truth is, I wanted to spend some time with Josie. At the ranch everyone has been watching us, and the same in town." He reached out and drew Josie to his side. "So when Josie needed to be in L.A. I offered to come along and help out. We thought if we came here we wouldn't have that pressure."

He felt Josie tense. "I think what Garrett left out is the fact that we aren't officially a couple." She turned those blue eyes toward him, and he suddenly wished for what he couldn't have.

"We're taking things slow," she added, not liking their made-up story.

Tori's dark eyes went back and forth between the two of them. "Yeah, like I believe that. Come on into the kitchen."

Garrett followed but took the chance to look around. The main living space was painted dark beige and had a sectional sofa in crimson. They passed a staircase that led to the second floor. The hall was tiled, but the rest of the floors were a dark hardwood. They walked through an archway into a big kitchen and family room area. The cupboards were painted a glossy cream color with colorful tiled counters.

"Wow, I really like your home. There's so much character."

Josie went straight to the large worktable in the family room with French doors leading to a patio. "That's the reason I bought the place, and it was a good investment at the time. It's been a lot of work." She smiled proudly. "Now that I know how to tape and mud drywall, I can do more remodeling."

"Or you can call your favorite handyman," he told her, and felt the heat spark between them.

"Hey, you two," Tori called.

They turned to Tori. "In case you've forgotten we've got a wedding to put together in two days. Isn't that the reason you came back?"

CHAPTER NINE

EARLY THE NEXT MORNING, there was little traffic on the 101 Freeway, so it had been a pleasant drive up from Los Angeles to Santa Barbara, especially with the springlike temperatures.

Occasionally, Garrett glanced at Josie, seated next to him in the car, but the conversation had been all but nil because she was either on her cell phone or working on her notes for the wedding later today.

Last night they hadn't talked much, either. They'd ordered pizza for dinner and discussed the details of the Santa Barbara wedding trip. Then Josie went up to her room, and Garrett went for a walk. Although the street was busy with traffic, he liked the older neighborhood. It seemed safe enough, but that could be the perfect cover for the ex-boyfriend, Dane. He still didn't feel good about leaving the two sisters alone with a crazy on the loose.

He thought about what Josie said to him a few

days ago. "We're not your problem." What if he wanted her to be?

He glanced across the car at Josie. This could all end up badly if he got his heart involved… again.

Garrett shifted in the driver's seat and concentrated on following the white cargo van with Slater Style embossed on the sides as they made their way through the coastal town into the hills and the Collins Family Rose Farm.

It was 7:00 a.m. when they drove up the steep road through the rose-covered hillsides toward a huge whitewashed barn. Standing in front was a group of workers, probably waiting for the next set of instructions.

"Good, the crew's here," Josie said more to herself than anyone else. "Looks like the tables and chairs have been delivered. And Mrs. Collins is here, too."

Practically before the car stopped, Josie grabbed her clipboard, was out the door and giving instructions to the crew. Then she took off again toward the older woman.

Garrett had trouble keeping up as he followed her toward the huge barn. He stood in awe of the hundred-year-old two-story structure as Josie talked to the mother of the bride. Using soothing hand motions, Josie assured the woman that nothing would go wrong on her daughter's special day.

"I assure you, Mrs. Collins, we'll have everything set up and ready hours before the first guests arrive for the ceremony."

The attractive older woman shook her head. "We could have had the wedding at a five-star hotel, but no, my daughter had to have it in a barn."

Josie's voice remained calm. "The renovations on this structure came out beautifully. Wait until you see it when I finish decorating the inside."

The mother of the bride didn't look convinced. "Nearly a hundred thousand dollars won't change the fact it's still a barn." She walked away and climbed into a golf cart and rode off toward the large house on the hill.

Garrett offered her an encouraging smile. "She's just nervous about the wedding."

Josie released a long sigh. "Welcome to my world."

He followed Josie inside the barn, but paused and looked around the huge open space. Along with a new concrete floor, a few horse stalls had been rebuilt along one side that would probably never see an animal. The beams overhead were massive and stained a rich walnut color.

Josie gave him a quick rundown on the Collins family history. The rose farm had been owned by them for over a hundred years. And great-granddaughter, Allison, wanted to be married in the barn her great-grandfather had built. "Of course after the renovations, it's perfect for what she wants."

"I think it's a great idea," Garrett said.

Before Josie could answer, her cell phone rang, and she quickly attached her Bluetooth to her ear and listened to her first crisis.

The portable bar collapsed, while workmen scurried around. Garrett got busy using his carpenter skills to get it fixed, then he went to look for Josie to get his next assignment. She directed him to stacks of chairs.

When that task was completed, he walked through the chaos to find Josie with Tori, and they were directing the florist about wrapping the greenery around the trellis that was placed in front of the open barn doors. It was where the ceremony would take place in the late afternoon.

Assured that Josie got her point across, she sent Tori off for another job, then made a call to the bride to remind her of the time for prewedding pictures. And that Megan would be there to help her.

Then she snagged Garrett to help dress the several round tables, adding burnt-orange-colored runners over the white linen. All the chairs had to be covered, too. By the time Garrett tied his last bow, he needed a break and grabbed two bottles of water and handed her one.

He stood next to Josie as they surveyed the area. The tables were now adorned with centerpieces of roses. Greenery had been draped over every stall, and baskets of multicolored flowers were everywhere. There was the sound of crystal and china being set out on long banquet tables. He was amazed how this production was all coming together.

"That was quite a workout," he admitted.

Josie was dressed in jeans and a sweatshirt, and her ponytail was askew. She took a hearty drink. He eyed her long slender neck as her throat worked to swallow. He felt the same familiar stirring he'd always had for her.

Her voice brought him back to the present. "It's the best workout, and you don't even need a gym membership." She glanced at her watch. "We need to get cleaned up. We have a wedding to go to."

Josie had to admit, Garrett had put in a hard morning without any complaint. She hadn't even had time to think about whether his coming this weekend was a good idea or not. She was just glad he'd been here to help out.

Back in the car, Josie directed Garrett to one of the guesthouses on the property that Mrs.

Collins had supplied the Slater Style crew. It was more convenient, so they didn't have to keep running up and down the hill to a hotel, especially to shower and change for the event. Catch was, she had to share it with Garrett.

About two hundred yards away from the Collins home and the barn, they found the small house nestled in a group of trees. They parked in the gravel driveway, and Josie used the key as Garrett and Tori brought in the bags.

"Oh, this is nice," Tori said.

Inside, the main room was surprisingly large with an open kitchen that had all the luxuries of home. There were two bedrooms, each with their own bath. Josie and Tori chose the larger of the bedrooms. "Garrett, you can use this one," she said, avoiding any eye contact with him. If things were different maybe… No, she couldn't go back there.

With a nod, he carried his bag into the first room with two single beds.

Tori stared at her twin. "I thought you said you two were a couple?"

"I said we're going slow, too. Besides, this isn't a getaway weekend. I'm working, so today is for my bride." Josie tossed her bag on the bed, hoping she convinced her sister. "Now, do you want to shower first?"

Tori watched her for a moment, as if she would

argue the point, but said, "Sure." She picked up her things and walked into the bathroom.

Josie sank down onto the king-size bed. Her sister could read her better than anyone, so she had to know that she and Garrett weren't a couple. She had no idea what they were. Old high school sweethearts? Friends?

Josie shook her head. *The wedding. Think about the wedding.* She wished now she'd changed places with Megan and taken the first bride duty.

Once she heard the shower turn on, she headed to the kitchen, wishing she could have a glass of wine, but that would have to wait until after the festivities.

She passed the living area and stopped short when she saw Garrett. He was bending down, getting something from the refrigerator, giving her a close-up view of his backside, slim hips and taut thighs. Then he stood, and she discovered he was shirtless.

She gasped and he quickly turned around. Oh, boy. His chest was impressive, too. Wide and well-developed and his arms…

"Is something wrong?" he asked.

"No. You…you just startled me. I didn't expect you…to be out here." *Stop rambling,* she told herself. "We don't have much time to get ready."

His gray eyes locked on hers. "Loosen up, Josie. We have time." He reached out and touched her cheek. "It's going to be perfect. You've done a great job. You have to be proud of this, and the business you've created."

She tried to speak, but her throat grew tight and she swallowed hard to clear it. It didn't help.

"I am proud of you. But I always knew you'd be a success at anything you attempted," he breathed as his head descended toward hers.

Even knowing what was about to happen wasn't wise, she couldn't move away as his mouth brushed over hers. She sucked in needed air, but before she could protest, he pulled back and gave her a smile.

"I should get back to my room before I get us both into trouble." He stepped around her and headed down the hall.

She sagged against the counter and watched the man walk away. The way her thoughts were going, she was already in trouble. Big trouble.

It was midnight, so Josie's job was officially over. The wedding ceremony had gone off with only minor mishaps, including a five-year-old ring bearer who suddenly refused to participate. No amount of bribing would make the boy go down that aisle.

The best man's toast revealed a little too much

about the groom's past, and the bride got a little too much cake on her face. Josie leaned against the stall gate next to the dance floor and watched the happy couple grooving to a fast-paced song, and smiled. Okay, she'd done a good job of putting this together, from the bride's spark of an idea to have her wedding on her family's estate.

She thought back to the project at the lodge. Could she put together a few wedding packages to help make it a successful venue and bring in money for the ranch?

"Looks like you can use this," a familiar voice said.

She looked over her shoulder and found Garrett holding two glasses of champagne. She accepted the crystal flute and took a sip of the Napa Valley vintage. Heavenly. She closed her eyes and savored the warm feeling the bubbly liquid gave her.

"You're a lifesaver."

She took a sip as she examined Garrett, dressed in his dark tailored slacks and wine-colored shirt with a dark print tie. Her heart went all aflutter gazing at the handsome man.

"At your service, ma'am."

Garrett leaned against the post on the stall and studied the beautiful woman in a basic black dress. Except there wasn't anything basic about Josie Slater. The knit material draped over her body, subtly showing off her curves. Her hair was swept up on top of her head, revealing her long graceful neck. Diamond studs adorned her sexy earlobes.

"I should have come to your rescue sooner, except I couldn't seem to catch up to you. I don't think anyone could."

"There's always a lot to do at these events. I'm actually off now, but until the bride and groom leave, anything can happen." She checked her watch. "I'm hoping that will be in the next thirty minutes."

The band ended one song and applause broke out in the crowd, then quickly died down when a ballad began, Al Green's "Let's Stay Together." Garrett didn't hesitate as he took the glass from Josie's hand and set it on the railing, then reached for her.

"I can't... I shouldn't, Garrett."

He shook his head as he drew her into his arms. "No one will even see us," he told her as they began to move to the music inside the privacy of the stall.

When he pulled her close, she didn't fight him. He bit back a groan, feeling her body pressed against him. He could barely move, afraid to disturb the moment. The familiarity of her scent, her touch, churned up so many emotions, emotions he thought had died long ago. He was wrong. So wrong. He'd never gotten over her.

When his thigh brushed Josie's, she drew a breath. He tightened his hold, knowing this moment in time was fleeting for both of them. He knew he shouldn't want this so much. It couldn't last. Soon they had to go back to reality and their different lives. Just seeing her in action today proved that.

Slowly the music faded, but he didn't release her. He closed his eyes, feeling her softness molded to him. They were a perfect fit. Hearing people approach, Josie pulled back, her eyes dark and filled with desire.

"I need to get back to work."

When she started to leave, he reached for her. "Josie…"

She stopped but didn't look at him. "This isn't a good idea, Garrett."

"It felt pretty good a few seconds ago."

Before she could speak, someone called to her. "I can't do this right now, Garrett. I need to get back to work." She pulled away and hurried off.

Garrett walked to the edge of the stall. "This isn't over, Josie."

It was after one in the morning before the caterers finished cleaning up and left the premises.

The band had packed up their equipment and driven off thirty minutes earlier.

The newlyweds had a formal send-off just after midnight, and the party finally began to wind down and the rest of the Collins/Brimley families went home, too. Josie pulled the sweater coat tighter around her shoulders to ward off the night's chill. She caught up with Tori and Megan while they finished packing up the Slater Style van.

"Thank you so much," she said and hugged them both. "Everything turned out wonderful."

"Wait until you get my bill," Tori teased, fighting a yawn.

"Then let's go to the cottage so we can get some sleep. Mrs. Collins said we can stay as late tomorrow as we want."

Tori shook her head. "I'm not staying. I'm going back with Megan."

"But the traffic," Josie said, trying to change her decision. She wasn't sure if she could handle Garrett as close as the next bedroom. "And what about Dane?"

"I'm not driving. And I haven't seen Dane in over a week. Besides, I'm going to spend the night with Megan."

"No need to stay with Megan, I'll go back, too. Give me fifteen minutes to pack up." She glanced around for Garrett. "I'm sure Garrett would be willing to drive back."

Tori took her sister's hand. "No, Josie. You stay here." She paused and pulled her away from the others for some privacy. "I've been watching you and Garrett dance around each other all day and this evening in the stall."

Josie released a breath. "That wasn't very smart of me."

"You need some time alone to figure out where to go with those feelings."

Josie knew that was the last thing she needed. Garrett could hurt her again. "I can't get involved with him again."

Tori hugged her. "Dear sister, that's the problem. You've never gotten uninvolved with the man. And if you look closely, he still has feelings for you. Maybe you should find out where it goes."

Josie shook her head. "This isn't a good idea. I can't let him hurt me again."

"How do you know that will happen? It's been nearly ten years. Maybe there's something there to build on, but at the very least you need closure." She kissed her, then started walking toward the van. "I'll see you tomorrow."

Josie watched Tori climb in, and soon they drove off. Her heart pounded in her chest as

Garrett walked toward her. Did she really want to get involved with Garrett again?

"It seems we have this knack for getting stranded together." He reached out and cupped her cheek, then leaned down and brushed a kiss over her mouth. She shivered at his touch. Oh, God, she ached for him.

He pulled back. His dark gaze said so much. "Do you want me to take you back to L.A., too?"

Darn the man, he was leaving this up to her. "No, I want to stay here tonight. With you."

Garrett's hand was shaking as he took Josie's and they made their way along the path that led to the small cottage with a single light on the porch. The rush of excitement from being with her was even stronger than all those years ago when he'd first met her. He still cared about her.

He took out the key and inserted it into the lock, then pushed open the door, allowing her to go inside first.

He followed then closed the door, but quickly found himself pushed up against the raised panels with Josie's hands wrapped around his neck. She pulled his head down to meet her hungry mouth and didn't stop there. She went to work on seducing him with her lips, hands and her body.

He broke off the kiss. "I take it you're glad we're staying."

"Don't get cocky, Temple, or I won't let you get to first base, let alone make all your dreams come true tonight."

Well, well! He couldn't help but grin, remembering that first base had been as far as he'd gotten while they'd dated in school. He quickly sobered, and leaned down to whisper in her ear, "I want to make your dreams come true."

His mouth brushed over hers, so gently, so softly she nearly groaned in frustration. She told herself this was crazy, but it felt too good. It always felt good with Garrett.

Josie shivered at his words. "Oh, Garrett," she breathed.

His lips found hers again, and he angled her mouth to deepen the kiss, letting her know how much he wanted her. When he released her, they were both breathing hard. "Let's continue this somewhere we'll be more comfortable." He swung her up in his arms and carried her down the hall into her room.

"Good idea." She kicked off her shoes as they went to her bedroom.

It was dark, only the light from the hall illuminated the room, helping to direct him to the king-size bed. He set her down and kissed her again and again. "I thought you'd appreciate the bigger bed, since my room has singles."

Josie looked around the room. Her sister had

straightened up the mess they'd left earlier with the rush to leave for the wedding. She looked back up at the man she'd wanted since the first day she'd met him in high school.

He leaned down and pressed his lips against her ear. "I want you, Josie Slater. More than you could ever imagine, but if you're having second thoughts…"

More like third and fourth, yet she reached out with shaky fingers to unbutton his dress shirt. With her heart beating wildly, she parted the material, and her hands came in contact with his chest. He sucked in a breath. "Only if you want to stop—"

His mouth came down hard on hers. This time slow and deeper, giving her his tongue and feasting on her until she was clinging to him. Her fingers tangled in his hair, holding him close. It left her no doubt what he wanted. The sensations that he created had her pressing against him as his hands worked the zipper at the back of her dress. Soon the soft fabric landed in a heap on the floor. Her pulse danced.

This time he sucked in a breath. "You are gorgeous." He dipped his head and kissed her. No man's touch had ever affected her like this.

"My turn," she said bravely. She pushed his shirt off those wide shoulders, then hungrily ran her fingers through the mat of dark hair that covered his beautiful chest. Next she used her lips to place kisses along his heated skin, causing him to tense.

"I'm not sure how much I can stand." He cupped her face and leaned down and kissed her. "I want you so much, Josie."

She looked into his eyes, seeing his need, his desire for her. "I want you, too, Garrett."

His mouth came down on hers, and true to his promise…he began to make her dreams come true.

CHAPTER TEN

IT WASN'T EVEN dawn yet, but Garrett was wide-awake. It might have something to do with the woman lying next to him. Last night had been incredible. Loving Josie had been only a dream, and now that dream had become a reality.

He wasn't naive enough to think she would wake up and want to continue what they'd started last night. But he had all morning to try and convince her. Even he wasn't sure how they could solve many of their problems. She had a life here, and she'd told him so many times that she didn't want to give it up. How could she give up a thriving business? He had a business, too, and so much more. There was his ailing father and a son to raise. Brody had to come first.

Josie moved beside him, then she rolled toward him, throwing her arm across his chest. He tensed, feeling her warm flesh against his, stirring him once again. He wanted her even more than he had all those years ago. He made the mistake then of giving up on her. There was no way he would do that again, not easily. Not when he knew Josie still had feelings for him.

He felt her cheek against his shoulder, her breast brushed his chest. Her legs tangled with his, inciting him further. Then her eyelashes fluttered and she finally opened them.

He froze and offered her a smile. "Hi, there."

She smiled back. "Hi, yourself."

She looked a little unsure and started to turn away. He wouldn't let her. Then he leaned down and opening his mouth against her throat, he kissed her, causing her to shiver. He wanted her to understand that whatever was happening, he wanted more than one night.

He raised his head and looked at her. "No hiding, Josie. Not after last night. You have to realize that there's still something between us."

She didn't say anything.

"Can you at least admit to that?"

"Okay, so you rocked my world. That doesn't mean it goes further than last night."

She was so stubborn. "It's not even up for discussion?"

"I thought we agreed that we had separate worlds, and there's no possible way we can combine them."

He felt the constriction in his chest. There had

to be a way for them to be together. "I don't want you to walk away again."

She hesitated. Wasn't that a good sign? "Garrett, we talked about this. Our lives are so different…"

"The hell with our lives, what about what we feel?" He placed her hand against his bare chest. "Feel my heart pound, Josie. Only you can make that happen."

Josie had tears in her eyes as she moved his hand and put it against her chest so he could also feel the rapid rhythm. "Ditto."

Garrett rolled her onto her back and captured her mouth in a hungry kiss. He felt her palm against his chest starting to push him away, but not for long. Her arms wrapped around his neck and brought him closer. When her mouth opened on a groan, he pushed his tongue inside, stroking and teasing her. Soon, his hands moved over her body, caressing her warm skin.

"Garrett…"

He looked at her as the morning sun began to slowly illuminate the bedroom. He could see the desire in her eyes and he touched her cheek. He'd never felt such closeness with anyone, only with Josie.

"I love it when you say my name, especially when I'm doing something to please you." He felt like a teenager again. "Tell me what you want, Josie Slater."

She arched her back as his hand cupped her breast. "You. I want you."

"You've always had me, Josie," he said as his mouth captured hers just as a cell phone began to ring. It was Josie's.

She sat up, holding the sheet against her, and reached for her purse on the table next to her side of the bed. She checked the caller ID.

"It's Tori." She punched the button. "Tori, what's wrong?" Garrett watched her expression change to panic. "Get out of there and call the police." Josie nodded as she listened. "Okay, we'll be home as soon as possible." She hung up and looked at Garrett. "Someone broke into my house and trashed the place."

The trip back from Santa Barbara was fast. Josie didn't argue with Garrett about his speed, knowing she only wanted to get to her sister. By the time they pulled up in front of her condo, Josie was out and running to her sister, who was standing on the small lawn.

Josie grabbed Tori close and felt her trembling. "Oh, Tori, I'm so glad you're safe." She shivered. "Thank God you were staying with Megan and not here."

Tori nodded at Garrett then back to her. "I'm so sorry about your house, Josie."

"Why are you sorry? You didn't do any of this."

She saw the tormented look in her twin's eyes. "If I'd only pressed charges against him before…"

"No! That's in the past, Tori. Dane's not going to get off free this time." She glanced around. "Where's Detective Brandon?"

"He's inside," Tori said. "But he wants us to wait out here."

"Too bad." Josie marched up the two steps and through the doorway.

She bit her bottom lip, trying to hold back the emotion as she glanced around the entry. All the work she'd put into her home and some crazy had broken in and destroyed it.

She couldn't hold back a gasp as her gaze roamed toward the living room, where furniture had been turned over, cushions were sliced with a knife and stuffing was scattered all around. Pictures had been destroyed and thrown to the floor. In their place on the walls were spray painted messages. Horrible words.

Garrett cursed. "They'd better have this creep and bully in custody," he said.

Teary-eyed, Tori shook her head. "Detective Brandon said until they find proof that Dane did this, they have to treat it like a random break-in. We're not to touch anything."

Just then Josie saw a uniformed officer coming down the hall. He had on a pair of rubber gloves and was carrying a plastic bag. She fought back her anger that someone was going through her personal things.

"It's going to be okay," she told Tori, but wasn't sure she believed it.

"How can you say that? Look at this place," Tori said, barely holding it together.

Garrett stepped forward. "These are just things, Tori. It's you we're worried about." When Tori nodded, he hugged her. "We'll get to the bottom of this," he promised her.

He turned to Josie and pulled her close, too. She stiffened, hating that she wanted his comforting embrace. In a few weeks Garrett Temple wouldn't be around for her to lean on. He'd be back in Montana and she'd be here. And once again, she'd have to learn to live without him.

Their moment of quiet was interrupted when a middle-aged man dressed in dark slacks and a white shirt and a tie under a nylon jacket that read LAPD walked into the room.

"Miss Slater." Detective Brandon nodded in greeting. "I'm sorry we have to meet again under these circumstances."

She was working to hold on to her composure. "Sorry, doesn't cut it, Detective. You know Dane Buckley is behind this. A random thief doesn't leave personal messages," she told him, and pointed to the wall.

The detective nodded in agreement. "But until we have proof who did this, I can't arrest him or anyone. We are bringing him in for questioning. We're also talking to your neighbors. Maybe they saw him around." He frowned. "We should be finished with photos and fingerprints by the end of the day, so you can call your insurance company and make arrangements to clean and paint the place."

Josie knew that new paint and furniture wouldn't erase this memory. How could she ever feel safe here again?

After exchanging goodbyes, the detective walked out the door, and Garrett followed him, but it was difficult to stay calm.

"Detective, tell me you aren't going to just push this case aside and wait for Buckley to strike again."

He saw the frustration in the man's eyes. "Like I said, we find some proof, and I'll do everything I can to get this predator off the street. If you want to help, I suggest you get both sisters away from here. This guy's message is clear. He wants revenge."

Garrett already knew that. "How would you feel if I bring in some outside help?"

The cop watched him. "As long as you don't interfere with the investigation or do anything illegal, I don't have a problem."

Garrett shook the officer's hand before he walked away. He took out his cell phone, not intending to stand by and let anything happen to Josie or Tori.

He needed someone he could trust. Brad Richards had helped him out before when someone hacked into his business computer system. He punched in the number and after the third ring it was answered. "McNeely Investigations."

"Hey, Brad, it's Garrett Temple."

There was a pause, then the ex-Special Forces soldier said, "What can I do for you, Garrett?"

"I need you to look into someone's past. Someone who preys on women."

"When and where do you need me?"

Two days later, after contacting the insurance company and scheduling the cleanup, Garrett had finally managed to get Tori and Josie on a noon flight back to Montana.

Josie had put on a brave front, but he knew she'd been frightened by this lunatic. He'd hoped that she would lean on him. Instead, she'd done everything she could to avoid coming near him.

She had stayed busy dealing with all the mess, trying to gather up their things to take back to Montana. He'd at least gotten them to move into a hotel, and then their agreement to come back to the ranch until Ana's wedding. There was no way he was going to leave them behind.

He was just happy Josie was returning with him, but his true wish was that they were still in Santa Barbara. Before her world had suddenly been turned upside down. Before reality invaded and threw yet another obstacle at them. Before she pulled away from him once again.

He drove under the archway to the Lazy S Ranch. The pastures were covered in layers of snow, but the roads had been cleared from the recent snowstorm. "We're almost home," he told them.

"This isn't my home," Tori murmured.

Garrett glanced in the rearview mirror. Tori was looking out the window.

It might not be her home any longer, but as long as Dane was on the loose they were in danger. He prayed both Tori and Josie would stay here for as long as it took for them to be safe again.

"It will be for the next few weeks."

He heard Tori's sigh. "As long as you don't tell anyone what happened, I'll stay."

He didn't like that deal. Everyone needed to be vigilant if a stranger showed up.

"Deal," he said, and looked at Josie. That meant she'd be going back, too. He honestly didn't want her to go. Would she even think about staying in Montana to give them a second chance? By the look of her body language, he had no chance at all.

Garrett pulled into the driveway and saw his dad's truck. He parked, then the front door opened and Brody came running out. He couldn't get out of the car fast enough. The bitter cold air stung his face, but he only saw his son.

"Dad!" The boy launched himself into his waiting arms. "You're home."

"I'm glad I'm back, too." He set his son down and pulled his jacket together to ward off the cold. "Did you have fun with Grandpa and Grandma Kirkwood?"

He nodded. "But I missed you."

Those were wonderful words to hear. "I've missed you, too, son."

Brody's attention went to the passengers. "Josie! You came back, too." He ran to her side of the car and hugged her. "Colt was afraid you might stay in California."

She ruffled the boy's hair. "No, I had to come back so I can get a video game rematch. You promised to teach me how to get to the next level." She directed him to the other side of the car. "Brody, this is my sister, Tori. She's going to be staying for a while."

"Hi, Tori. I can teach you how to play video games if you want."

"Great to meet you, Brody."

Garrett got the suitcases out of the trunk and urged the group toward the house. "Hey, let's take this conversation inside where it's warm."

Brody ran up ahead calling back to the sisters, "Yeah, Kathleen baked a cake."

Josie stopped on the porch and waited as Tori stepped across the threshold and into the entry. She was pretty sure she knew what was going through her sister's head. It was hard not to think about the past years here along with the father who'd ignored them. It had been a cold existence for the four girls growing up here.

Josie looked down the hall and saw Colt walking toward them. His gait was slow and maybe not as steady as it should be, but there'd been improvement since Josie had first come home over three weeks ago.

She watched her sister's reaction. Would she accept the changes in this man? Even Josie had been leery that maybe the cold, distant man would return. Over the past weeks, she'd seen changes in Colt. She was willing to give him a chance to be the father he'd said he wanted to be, but Tori had to make her own decision.

"Vittoria." He came to her and without hesitation reached out and took her hand in his. "I'm so glad you're home."

"Hello, Colt. I'm glad to see you're doing well."

Josie could see how hard it was for her sister to hold back the tears.

"It gets better each time one of my daughters comes home," Colt told her.

She shook her head. "I'm only staying until Ana's wedding." She glanced around. "Speaking of Ana, where is my big sister?"

"She's working at the high school," a familiar male voice answered.

They turned to see Vance coming toward them. "She'll be home soon. Hi, Tori. It's good to see you again."

Tori smiled. "Good to see you, too, Vance. How are you surviving the wedding plans?"

He grinned. "Anything Ana wants. I just hope it happens soon before she realizes I'm not such a great catch."

"Oh, I think Ana knows what a good man you are." Tears welled in her eyes. "And you've always treated her well."

"I love her and wouldn't intentionally do anything to hurt her."

Tori nodded. "Good." She stepped back as another woman hurried in.

"Kathleen," Tori cried as the older woman took her into her welcoming arms.

"Another of my babies came home." She wiped her eyes. "Praise the Lord."

Tori grinned and looked at the older woman. "I can't tell you how much I've missed you."

"I know, child. I always enjoyed your cards and presents." Those kind hazel eyes searched Tori's face. "Your heart is sad. I'm glad you came home."

Even Josie had to wipe away tears.

Tori nodded. "Would anyone mind if I went upstairs and rested?"

"Of course not," everyone chimed in. Tori looked toward the staircase. "Which room?"

"I put your suitcase in your old bedroom," Garrett told her.

Josie felt her cheeks redden and rushed on to explain. "Garrett and Brody stayed during the blizzard two weeks ago."

Tori gave her a knowing smile and walked off with Kathleen.

Josie looked across the entry at Garrett. He turned his gray gaze on her, and she felt that familiar jolt. He was a hard man to resist. She'd already let her defenses drop, but she couldn't let it happen again. She was L.A. bound.

* * *

At eleven o'clock the house was quiet, and everyone had settled in for the night. In his room, Colt stood in the darkness by the window. If there was one thing he enjoyed about having to move his bedroom downstairs, it was the view. He could see the entire compound, the corral, the barn. He could keep an eye on the operation.

He looked out at the foreman's cottage and saw the lights go off. He smiled to himself. Ana and Vance were probably heading to bed. His oldest daughter had no qualms about staying with the man she planned to marry. Colt didn't, either. Life was too short to waste; love was too fleeting.

Regrets. Colt closed his eyes against the memories. He had too many regrets to count. The biggest mistake had been turning away from his daughters when they needed him the most. No more.

Three of his four daughters were home now. Not for long, and somehow he needed to prove to them that he was worth the risk. Okay, Ana was happy with Vance, and they would be living close. Josie was a different story. He'd been watching the sparks fly between her and Garrett. He doubted that his girl was going to give the man a second chance easily. But he had hopes that they would work things out.

Then there was Tori. Something bad had happened to her in California. He didn't know what it was, and she didn't trust him enough to tell him. He hated to see the pain in her beautiful dark eyes. He had to help her.

Suddenly, fatigue hit him hard, and Colt closed the window shades and walked to his bed. When would he get his energy back? When would he get his life back? He opened the buttons on his shirt and stripped it off his shoulders and tossed it on the chair. He liked that his arm had regained strength. His therapy with Jay was tough, but it was paying off. He had good muscle tone.

He went for the button fly on his jeans when he caught a familiar scent. Roses. He glanced toward the door and saw a small figure standing there. He blinked once, then again.

"Who is it?" he asked, afraid to know. "Who are you?"

"Colt…" a woman's voice said.

He froze. No. It couldn't be. He felt his heart hammering in his chest as the figure stepped into the dim lamplight. The slender figure was dressed in black. Her hair was long, reaching her shoulders. Although her face was in the shadows, he knew her eyes were almond-shaped and as black as midnight. He forced himself to take a breath. "Lucia…"

CHAPTER ELEVEN

AFTER A RESTLESS NIGHT, Josie slept in later than usual. Tori was already up and gone from the room. Not surprising, since she'd heard her sister tossing around in the other bed most of the night. Not that she'd blamed her for feeling uneasy after the break-in. For now, they were both safe here. But how long could they hide out at the ranch when their lives were in California?

Of course, Montana had Garrett Temple. And now, after his visit to L.A., she knew firsthand how he would never fit into her life, any more than she'd fit into his. No matter how incredible their night together had been, it had to be a onetime thing.

Not that he would ever ask her for more. He had a child to think about. She smiled. Brody was a sweet boy, but his home was here, too.

She sighed. No more dreams about Garrett. She needed to focus on Ana's wedding, and enjoy her remaining time here with her family.

She thought about Colt. She'd been surprised how much she liked spending time with him. He'd even taken an interest in her life and her work. The Colt Slater she'd remembered never had time for his daughters.

Could her father change that much?

After showering and dressing, Josie went downstairs to find Ana, Tori and Colt waiting for her in the kitchen.

"Good, you're finally awake," Ana said. "We want to drive out to the lodge. Garrett and Vance are already there finishing up any last-minute details. Also, Colt and Tori haven't seen the place."

"Do you think I have time for some coffee and toast?"

"Of course you do," Kathleen said, filling her cup.

As much as Josie wanted to delay the inevitable, she had to go. After her quick breakfast, they jumped into Colt's pickup and headed out to the river.

Ana chattered most of the way about wedding details. Josie took notes and asked even more questions, trying to concentrate on her job rather than on seeing Garrett again. When Ana pulled up to the construction site, Vance and Garrett's trucks were there, and her heart began to race.

"Good, the guys are already here. I can't wait

to see all the finishing touches to the place." She turned to Colt. "Oh, wait until you see it, Tori, Dad. It's beautiful."

They climbed out and helped Colt while he used his cane to get over the plywood walkway toward the wide porch. Josie made more notes about some minor landscaping needs.

Colt stopped and gazed at the two-story log structure. "Land sakes, she's a beauty." He looked overwhelmed. "I'm glad Ana didn't listen to an old man's rantings and got this place built."

Ana grinned. "Actually, the lodge was Josie's idea."

"Well, I give you all the credit for coming up with ideas to help out. I'm so grateful."

They finally reached the front door, and Ana paused and brushed her ebony hair off her shoulders. "It's been a while since I've been here. Vance said he didn't want me to see it until it was completed. Dad, welcome to River's Edge Lodge." She swung open the doors, and the group walked across the threshold.

Ana let out a gasp as her gaze moved around the large open room with the massive floor-to-ceiling river rock fireplace. There were honey-oak hardwood floors and the far wall was all windows, overlooking the river and mountain range.

Tears came to Ana's eyes. "Oh, it's perfect."

"That's good to hear," a familiar man's voice said.

Josie swung around to find Vance and Garrett were right behind her. The handsome men wore tool belts to let the others know they'd been working this morning.

Ana ran to her man. Josie stood in her place, hating the fact she wished she could go to Garrett. Whoa. *He isn't yours to run to.*

"It's perfect," Ana said.

"Then it's worth all the work we put in." Vance looked at Colt. "How do you like it?"

Her father shook his head. "What's not to like?" He glanced at Garrett. "Thank you for all you've done."

"You're welcome, but your future son-in-law and Josie put in a lot of work, too."

Vance turned to Ana. "I know Josie worked really hard, and Garrett also logged in time he didn't bill us for. These two put in a long few weeks to make sure it was finished for our wedding."

Ana looked at her and mouthed, "Thank you."

Josie didn't want any praise. "Hey, I'm the maid of honor, and besides, we need to get this place rented to start making some money."

"Well, then, let's start booking the place," Ana said.

Tori jumped in. "We'll need to take a few pictures for the website and then we can begin to advertise River's Edge Lodge." She turned to Colt. "Do we have your approval?"

Josie could see the emotion on her father's face. "My approval? But I didn't put in a lick of the work."

Ana stepped forward. "The Lazy S is your ranch, Dad. Vance and I had power of attorney while you were recovering, but you're still the head of this family, and we make decisions together."

Colt nodded as tears filled his eyes. "Let's have a wedding, and then start taking reservations."

Ana clasped her hands together. "I have another question to ask you, Dad." Ana paused a moment. "Would you give me away?"

The room grew silent. Josie glanced at Garrett. He caught her gaze, and she couldn't seem to look away until her father answered, "Oh, Analeigh, I'd be honored." He took her hand. "But I hate to give you away since I just found you."

"I think Vance would be willing to share me with you. And we'll be living practically outside your door in the foreman's house." She glanced at Vance and smiled. "Until we get our new home built this spring."

Colt tapped his cane. "I wish I could do more to contribute to the operation."

Vance patted him on the back. "Come spring, Colt, I have no doubt you'll be back on a horse. Until then we'll help each other because that's what families do."

Colt nodded.

Vance tugged on Ana's arm. "Come on, we want to show you the rest of the place."

Vance and Ana took Tori and Colt up the stairs.

Garrett stayed back watching Josie taking some notes for the wedding beside the big window. She'd been doing her best to keep her distance ever since they returned to Montana. They'd spent four days together while in California, and then yesterday they'd gone their separate ways. He'd found he'd missed her. Lying in bed last night, he couldn't sleep as memories of her flooded his head. He knew these feelings he had for her complicated his life. It would be disastrous if let himself fall in love with her again.

He wasn't listening to common sense when he walked up to her. "How'd you sleep last night?"

She swung around, looking startled. "Oh, fine. I was pretty tired after the flight."

He reached out and touched her cheek. "I miss you, Josie. Being with you in Santa Barbara was incredible."

He watched her eyes darken and knew she'd been just as affected by what happened between them as he was.

She closed her eyes a moment. "It was, but we can't go back there again."

He knew that. He heard the voices upstairs. "Maybe we could go somewhere and talk about that."

Josie shook her head. "Garrett, we had our night. A night that we should have had as teenagers, but we aren't those kids anymore."

Years ago, they'd planned to wait until they were married to have sex. He forced a smile. "We still have feelings for each other."

"I think we always will." She sighed and glanced away. "We have different lives now. I'm going back to L.A., and you're staying here because it's where you belong...with your son."

He felt tightness in his chest as his heart lodged in his throat. He was losing her again. He should be used to her rejection, but it still hurt like hell. "You're right. Brody has to be my main focus." Wanting her had made him forget that. "Then I guess there's nothing more to say."

Josie avoided his gaze. "I guess not." She finally looked at him. "If things were different—"

He raised his hand to stop from hearing her regrets. The familiar ache brought him back to all those years ago. He felt the pain again.

"There's no need to explain. It's been over for a lot of years. It's best we stop now before—"

All at once the rest of the group appeared above them along the open staircase and started down the steps.

"We're all going to lunch at the Big Sky Café," Vance announced. "You two want to join us?"

"Sure," Josie said, lacking enthusiasm.

Garrett couldn't be with Josie and keep pretending. He looked at his watch. "I'll have to pass. I need to check on another job in Dillon."

After another round of thanks to him, the Slaters started out the door. Josie was the last to leave. She turned and looked at him. "This is for the best, Garrett. You'll see."

He nodded and she left. "Yeah, we'll always have Santa Barbara." Why wasn't that enough?

It was Thanksgiving morning, and Garrett had to start the celebration by breaking the bad news to his son. They weren't going to the Slaters' today.

"But we were invited," Brody said. "Why can't we go?" The child was close to tears.

"There's been a change in plans, son. They have family home from California and they should spend time together."

Brody jumped up from the kitchen table. "It's

not fair. I wanted to be with Josie and Tori. We were going to play video games."

"I'll play games with you."

"I don't want to play with you." The boy glared at him. "What did you do to make Josie mad?"

He was taken aback by Brody's comment. "I didn't do anything."

"Yes, you did. You always made Mom mad."

Whoa, where did that come from? "It wasn't intentional, son. People argue sometimes."

The child didn't look convinced, so Garrett went on to say, "We're not Josie's family, and Josie, Tori and Ana need time with their dad."

"I don't believe you," the boy shouted before he ran from the room.

Garrett started to go after him, but walked to the kitchen window and looked out. They both needed to cool off. It was obvious he and his son had more to work through. Worse, Brody was getting too attached to Josie. When she went back to L.A., he knew his son would be hurt.

"You okay, Garrett?"

He turned to see his father and nodded.

Nolan Temple walked over to him. "Kids say things because they're hurt and disappointed."

"Maybe he's right," he began. "I wasn't the best husband."

"But you were always the best father to that

boy," Nolan countered. "He had a rough time with the divorce, then his mother's passing not even a year ago, and the move here. Give him time."

"What if I do it all wrong?"

"Just keep loving that boy." His dad nodded. "But don't let your marriage to Natalie keep you from moving on."

Garrett sighed. He didn't want to think about his ex-wife or their bad years together. "I wasn't the man she needed. As you saw with Brody's attitude, I caused a lot of damage."

"Don't be too quick to take all the blame, son. It takes two to make a marriage work." Nolan shook his head. "I'm sorry. I won't speak ill of the dead."

His father changed the subject. "When Josie showed up, I was kind of hoping you two would find each other again. You kind of gave Colt and I some hope when you went off to L.A. together."

He'd given himself some hope. Garrett shrugged, not wanting to rehash this. He hoped he'd been able to accept the fact that once again she'd leave and he'd stay here. "And she's returning to L.A."

His father nodded. "Have you asked her to stay?"

Garrett thought back to the wedding in Santa

Barbara. He'd seen Josie at work. "She has her business there. I have my work here. We have the ranch and our home, and there's Brody."

"I guess you've thought this out."

"Look, Dad, I'm not that boy she left behind years ago. I have to think of my son. I'm not going to chase after someone who doesn't want me."

"Who said she doesn't want you?"

"She did, okay," he answered a little too loud. "Sorry."

His father reached out and placed a hand on his arm. "It's hard to give you advice, son. From the minute I saw your mother, I fell in love." His father's gaze settled on him. "I don't have any regrets except I didn't have enough time with her. Twenty-five years seems like a lifetime, but it's not. I miss her every day. I wake up missing her, and I go to bed every night missing her."

Garrett had always envied his parents and the affection they showed each other. He smiled. "You two were so loving."

"Josie and her sisters haven't been as lucky with their parents. Colt might be seeing the error of his ways since his stroke, but those girls never had a mother and father who were there for them growing up. It makes trust hard."

Garrett didn't say anything. He knew, outside of Kathleen, Josie and her sisters had been on their own growing up. He recalled the teenage Josie who was afraid of the passion they shared. Then he'd gone away to college and left her behind.

Garrett shook his head. No, he needed to move away from the past. How could he do that when all he wanted was in his past?

Josie never remembered having a Thanksgiving like this. The kitchen was filled with her sisters helping Kathleen prepare the large turkey. Laughing and joking went on all the while they worked on the food prep. It was almost the best Thanksgiving ever. Then she thought about Garrett, knowing he wasn't coming today because of her. It was for the best. In the long run, he would thank her.

Ana walked into the room carrying a large leather album.

"Did you find the silverware?" Josie asked.

Ana held up the book. "No, but look what I found."

Josie and Tori went to the table where Ana laid out the book. Ana sat down, and the twins looked over her shoulder. Her sister gasped as she turned to the first page that showed a young Ana. "That's me!"

Josie smiled as she looked at the toddler in her

little cowgirl outfit and bright red boots and hat. "Oh, weren't you cute."

Ana turned to the next page and saw the twins, side by side wrapped in pink blankets. "Gosh, we look so much alike," Tori said. "I don't know who is who."

Ana pointed at the photo. "This is you, Josie, and this one is you, Tori."

They both stared at their older sister. "What? I was there so I know this. Our mother always put Tori on the left side because you, Josie, would fuss if she didn't."

"You always liked being the boss, even back then," Tori said.

Ana turned to the next page and they all froze. There was a large picture of Lucia and Colton Slater staring back at them. "Oh, my, I didn't think Colt kept any of her."

"We can't even say her name?" Tori asked. "It's Lucia."

Josie studied the beautiful woman in the portrait, their mother. She could barely remember the woman with the long black hair that smelled like flowers. She and Tori had only been three years old, and Marissa had been a year old when their mother left the family.

In the picture Ana was standing next to Colt, and the twins were in between them and Lucia held a toddler in her arms. "That's Marissa."

"There are so few baby pictures of her," Ana said.

"Maybe that's the reason she became a photographer," Tori said.

Ana looked at Josie. "Have you talked to her recently?"

"No, I tried before we left L.A. I wanted her to know we'd be out of town. Have you spoken to her?"

"Just once," Ana admitted. "I wanted to make sure she's coming to the wedding, and I hoped she'd come early for Thanksgiving."

Josie thought about all the times she'd called Marissa. San Diego was less than three hours away, but somehow they couldn't seem to get together. "What was her excuse this time?"

"That she has to photograph a big magazine layout. I asked her if she'd do the pictures for my wedding. She's going to try to make it. That's all I can ask." Ana got another dreamy look. "My sisters home. That would be a perfect day."

Not so perfect for Josie, not with having to spend the entire day with Garrett. All she had to do was get through the rehearsal dinner and the wedding before she could cut her ties with Garrett for good. She'd done it before; she could do it again. She just couldn't come back, knowing he'd be here, reminding her of what she couldn't have.

At least she didn't have to see him today, but

found she was disappointed that he and Brody weren't coming to Thanksgiving dinner.

There was a knock on the kitchen door, and Ana went to answer it. "Garrett. Oh, good, you've changed your mind about dinner."

He looked upset. "No, but I was hoping I'd find Brody here."

Josie felt a sudden panic. "No, he hasn't been here."

He removed his hat and ran his fingers through his hair. "He was upset with me for changing our dinner plans. He went to his room, but I discovered he took off on his bike. I was hoping he came here."

Josie gasped. "Garrett, we're over two miles from your house."

He shook his head. "Not if you take the shortcut along the river. Since the weather is so mild that road is pretty clear. It's the way I think he'd go." He started off the back stoop and grabbed his horse's reins. "I've got to go find him."

Dear God. Josie began to shake. "Then let's all go looking for him," she said.

Ana picked up the phone and dialed. "Vance is in the barn. I'll have him saddle up some horses."

"Have him saddle a mount for me, too," Josie said. "I'm going." This man came after her when she'd gotten lost. She had to help him find his son.

Dinner forgotten, the sisters grabbed warm coats and hats, then headed down to the barn. Ana's Blondie was saddled along with Vance's Rusty. Jake had a gentle mare, Molly, ready for Josie.

They had daylight in their favor, but still nightfall came fast in November. They had to find the child because a freeze warning was predicted for tonight.

Temple and Slater land bordered each other, but that left a lot of land to cover.

"My three men are fanned out along the bank on our side," Garrett said. "I thought Brody might show up here since this was where he wanted to come today."

"Is there anywhere else he might go, a special place?" Vance asked.

"I've talked to him about the river and the old cabin. I thought I explained we'd have to wait to go there until spring."

The riders were all given an area to search, and equipped with cell phones. Josie was going with Garrett, whether he wanted her to or not. "We're going to find him, Garrett."

He didn't say anything.

"He's a smart boy," she told him, praying that she was right, realizing how much she cared about the child.

Josie saw the pain on Garrett's face. She wished she could comfort him.

"Too smart for his own good," he blurted out. "Wait until I get…" He didn't finish the thought, just kicked his heels into Pirate's sides and took off.

She rode after him, knowing nothing else mattered but getting the child and his father back together.

An hour had passed, and the homestead cabin had been checked, but was found empty. Garrett was about to go out of his mind. "Dear God, where would he go?"

The wind had picked up, and the daylight was growing dim as clouds moved in.

Garrett looked ahead and side to side, knowing he had to phone the sheriff and get help in the air. Then he saw a shiny object flash in the sunlight. He rode closer and saw Brody's chrome bike just a few yards from the river. "It's his bike."

Josie climbed off her horse and reached for her cell phone to call Vance. "We found the bike, but no Brody." She gave her location as she led her horse along the rocky bank of the wide river behind Garrett.

"He's close by, Garrett. I just know it."

They walked about a quarter mile calling

Brody's name. That was when she heard the sound. She stopped Garrett. "I heard him."

Again the sound of Brody's voice. She dropped the horse's reins and took off toward the big tree and found the boy sitting against it. "Brody!" she cried and hurried to him.

Garrett passed her and got to the boy's side and reached for him. "Son, it's okay. We're here."

"It hurts, Dad." The boy was fighting tears. "Really bad. I slipped on that big rock by the river. I couldn't ride my bike home."

Garrett quickly examined his arm, then his shoulder. "It's going to be all right, son. Just hang in there for a few minutes and we'll get you some help."

Josie took Garrett's place next to Brody and took the boy's hand. "It's okay, Brody. Your dad's here. He'll take care of you."

Garrett pulled out his phone and called to have someone bring a truck. He looked at Josie, raw emotion showing on his face.

She looked up at him with those big eyes. "He's safe now, Garrett." She let her own tears fall. "Brody is safe."

CHAPTER TWELVE

THEY LEFT THE emergency room two hours later, after the doctor's diagnosis.

Brody had a hairline clavicle fracture. It wasn't a complete break, so the healing time would be shorter with less chance of losing any movement in his arm. Garrett breathed a sigh of relief.

After his son's arm had been put into a sling to keep his shoulder immobile, they headed back to the Slater house to drop off Josie and get Nolan.

It had been at Brody's insistence that she go along with him. And he was glad she'd been there to calm his son.

It was dark by the time Garrett pulled up, but before anyone got out of the truck, family filed out of the house. Brody was out of the vehicle before he could stop him.

After hugs all round, Ana coaxed them. "Come on, Josie, Garrett. We have Thanksgiving to celebrate."

Josie saw that Garrett wasn't happy as everyone went inside ahead of them. "I know you're still upset about what happened to Brody, but now is not the time."

Garrett shook his head and started to speak, then stopped. He walked back to the truck and turned around. "I could have lost him today. What if we hadn't found him?"

Josie went to him, feeling his pain. "Oh, Garrett, there are so many what-ifs, but what really happened today is your son made a mistake in judgment. But he's safe now, and he's going to be sitting down to Thanksgiving dinner with you."

He turned to her. Even in the darkness, she could see his tears. "This is hard. I'm so angry with him, but all I want to do is hold him close and protect him from all harm. I didn't do that today."

Josie tried to stay back, but she, too, had been terrified of losing Brody. She felt her own tears. "I'm not an expert, but I think you did everything right. You're a wonderful dad, Garrett." She went into his arms and hugged him close. It seemed the most natural thing to do.

Thanksgiving dinner was a joyous event, something that Josie had never experienced in the Slater house. Everyone was seated at the large dining room table, her father at the head and

Kathleen at the opposite end. Having the Temple family here added so much more to this day, more than she should allow herself to dream about. Although Nolan, Garrett and Brody had become a part of her life, it wouldn't be for much longer.

She glanced at the eight-year-old boy. Brody didn't seem to mind the discomfort in his shoulder. He was going to have a great story when he returned to class on Monday.

She turned her attention to Garrett, seated across from her. He looked tired, and there were still worry lines on his forehead. Again, she wanted to comfort him, and that was a mistake. Only days ago, they'd decided it was best to stay away from each other. Now look at them—they were acting like one big happy family.

Brody's laughter filled the room. "This is the best Thanksgiving ever," he said.

Garrett disagreed. "You might not think so when you receive your punishment for your stunt today."

The boy looked embarrassed as he glanced around the table. "I'm sorry that I caused so much trouble and spoiled everybody's Thanksgiving." He glanced at his father. "Did I say it right, Dad?"

Josie saw Garrett's pride. "You did it perfect, son. I'm proud of you for taking responsibility."

The boy perked up. "Do I get less punishment now?"

Everyone laughed, and Kathleen stood. "You better come with me, young man, and help me cut some pies. You can put on the whipped cream."

Colt called to the housekeeper. "Kathleen, could you hold off on dessert for about fifteen minutes?"

She nodded and took the boy's hand, and they walked into the kitchen.

Colt looked around the table. "I need to say a little something." He cleared his throat. "First of all, I'm very thankful that my daughters are here, also Vance and my friends—some old." He nodded to Wade. "Some new." He saluted Nolan and Garrett. "I'm not going to sugarcoat how bad things were through those years. If I apologize every day for the rest of my life, it still wouldn't make up for the hurt my daughters have lived through. I'm not going to make excuses... I am just going to say I'm sorry. I love you all, and I hope in time you girls can forgive me."

Josie felt the tears start. She glanced at her twin and saw the same. Vance put his arm around Ana and pulled her close.

"I made a vow when I was in the hospital that if I was given a second chance, I'd do whatever it takes to try and make it up to you girls."

He sighed and pulled out an envelope from his pocket. "I need to start with some honesty. This here is a twenty-five-year-old letter…from your mother."

Ana gasped. Josie froze, not wanting to feel anything. She glanced at Tori.

"It was sent along with the divorce papers. At first I was so angry, I nearly threw it away. Then I decided to save it until you girls got older. I honestly forgot about it and just found it the other day."

"Why even tell us about it?" Tori threw out. "Bring up memories about a woman who abandoned us? I don't want to hear anything she had to say."

Garrett felt uncomfortable and started to get up and leave the room, but Colt asked him to stay.

"You'll understand in a minute," Colt told him.

"I opened it because I wanted to protect you all." He glanced at Ana. "The last thing I want is for your mother to hurt you any more than she already has."

Josie didn't want to feel anything for a woman she barely knew. She didn't even care enough about her own children to stick around. "We don't need her letter now. Her leaving us says it all."

Ana gripped Vance's hand. "Do you want us to read the letter? Open all those wounds again?"

Colt glanced around the table. "I blame myself for not showing this to you before. My main reason is, as I told you, I wanted to be honest with you girls. So I'm leaving the decision up to you."

"I don't want to hear her tell us stuff just to ease her conscience," Tori said.

Colt sighed. "Look, I still have no idea why she left. For years I was selfish enough to think it was all about me. I think I was wrong.... So maybe you should read the letter and judge for yourself."

Garrett followed Colt, Vance and the family lawyer, Wade Dickson, into the office. His dad took charge of Brody, and they were watching a video in the Slaters' family room. The sisters disappeared upstairs to discuss the mysterious letter.

Garrett needed to be home with his son tucked into his bed, but he couldn't help thinking about Josie and the letter she had to deal with.

After shutting the door, Colt made his way to the desk chair. "Honestly, I had forgotten about that letter."

"Maybe it should have stayed forgotten," Vance said. "None of the girls need to be reminded their mother left them."

"I know, but let me explain something first."

He looked at Vance, then to Garrett. "I trust you two not to say anything to them just yet."

"You're asking a lot," Vance said. "I'm marrying your daughter in less than two weeks. I don't keep anything from her."

Garrett had no idea why he was here. "All we can promise is we'll hear you out, and then decide." He didn't want Josie hurt, either.

Colt nodded. "At first I thought it was the medication." He looked at Vance. "At the hospital after my stroke, someone came into my room late one night. She looked like Lucia."

"It probably was the meds," Vance told him. "They wanted you to rest and heal."

"I thought the same thing," Colt said. "But it happened again when I went into the rehab facility." He hesitated. "And then again when I returned home."

Garrett leaned forward. "Are you saying Lucia was here in this house?"

He nodded. "I'm as sure as I can be that the woman was in my room two nights ago."

"You talked to her?" Vance asked, looking skeptical.

"No, but she spoke to me. She said my name."

"What did you say to her?"

"When I said her name, she smiled. It made me angry, and I told her to get out. I turned around but when I looked again, she was gone."

Garrett wasn't sure what to think. "Do you think she's come back because she wants something? Money? Her daughters?"

Colt shook his head and looked at his friend, Wade. "I don't know. And it wasn't until I started looking at old pictures that I remembered the letter." He shook his head. "I knew I couldn't keep it from the girls. I want to be completely honest with them."

Vance began to pace then asked, "How could she get onto the ranch with no one knowing?"

Colt looked tired. "Hell, I don't know. And since I'm the only one who's seen her, I'm probably just going crazy." He waved a hand. "Maybe you should forget I said anything."

"No," Garrett said. "I think we need to check into it." He turned to Colt. "Do you know where Lucia went all those years ago?"

Colt shook his head. "Even though she was estranged from her family, I assumed she went back to Mexico." He got up and went to the wall safe and used the combination to open it. He pulled out a manila envelope and brought it back and tossed it on the desk. "Here are the divorce papers and the last correspondence we had through our lawyers."

He looked at Garrett. "Do you think your friend the P.I. can find out where Lucia is now?"

Vance put his hand on the papers. "Whoa, we aren't going to spoil Ana's wedding. She deserves her day."

Colt nodded. "Of course she does, and so do you. We can hold off with this until after the holidays."

Garrett nodded. Once again, he was getting involved in Josie's life. "I think the girls should decide if they want to find their mother."

Upstairs, the three sisters sat in Ana's room on the big bed with the letter. It was still in the envelope because a decision couldn't be made about what to do.

"What can she do to us now?" Josie asked. "The woman hasn't been in our lives for years." She glanced at Tori. "Besides, we barely remember her."

"I remember her," Ana said. "I loved her so much, I wanted to die after she left." Her voice was a hoarse whisper. "I never understood why she left and never even said goodbye." She took the letter. "Yes, I want to know what she wrote us. What we did that made her walk away from her family."

Ana got up from the bed and took out a single piece of paper from the yellowing envelope. She took a breath and released it, then read,

"'To my *bambinas,* Analeigh, Josefina, Vittoria and Marissa.

It is so hard to have to say these words to you, but I must. I cannot stay and be your mother any longer. It's not because I don't love you all, it's because I do. So I must leave you for a while. I'm needed back in Mexico to be with my family.

Please, know that I will think about you every day and pray that someday I will be able to return to you. For now, take care of your papa, and never forget me.

I vow, no matter how, I will find my way back to my *niñas.*

Love, Mama'"

Ana swallowed hard. "Oh, God. It sounds as if she didn't want to leave."

Josie wasn't so sure. "What else could she say? And where has she been all these years? Surely, if she wanted to come back, she would have been here before now. I don't want to do this." She got up from the bed and started to walk away.

"Wait, Josie," Ana called.

Josie turned around. "What?"

"Do you want to pursue this?"

"No! I don't know. Can we just wait a little while? I can't face this right now."

Ana nodded and said, "We'll decide after the wedding and the holidays."

All the sisters agreed, and Josie walked out of the room, her emotions in turmoil. She didn't need another rejection. Then a thought struck her. What if she wasn't even alive? Dear, God. What if Lucia Slater had died and she couldn't come back to them?

Trembling, she sank down on the top step, unable to stop the tears. She hated being weak. Her mother never mattered before. Why now? She'd never had her in her life. Why did she want her so badly now?

"Josie…"

She looked up from her perch on the step and saw Garrett. She saw the compassion in his eyes and knew she couldn't hold it together any longer.

"Oh, Garrett," she cried and went into his open arms. "She said she loved us. But she left anyway."

Garrett cupped the back of Josie's head and held her against his shoulder. She was heartbroken, and he couldn't help her. He couldn't stop her pain. "I'm here, Josie. I'll help you through this."

Suddenly, she pulled back and wiped at her tears. "I'm fine."

Garrett felt her pull away, both physically and

emotionally. "There's nothing wrong with leaning on someone, Josie. I want to be there for you."

She shook her head. "You'll go away. Everybody always goes away." She got up and hurried down the hall to her bedroom.

Garrett started to go after her, but knew she wasn't ready to listen. "I'm not going anywhere, Josie. Not this time."

He was going to figure out a way for them to be together. He wouldn't lose her again.

Another week had gone by, and Colt had filled his days with his therapy routine so he could be strong enough to walk Ana down the aisle at her wedding.

He felt fatigued as he looked out the window of his room. Had that been the reason for his confusion, for imagining the mystery woman in his room last week?

Was this part of the brain damage from his stroke? All he wanted to do was rebuild a relationship with his daughters, and so far he'd caused more problems. Vance was right. He should have waited until after the ceremony to dredge up the past.

Colt closed his eyes. He hated remembering back to that time. The years of misery without the woman he loved, but there had been years of joy with her, too.

"Oh, Lucia. What have you done? If you were to come back, do you realize the problems you'd create?" Dear God, for a long time after Lucia had left, he would have sold his soul to have her back in his life again.

"I was hoping you'd let me explain," a familiar voice said.

He sucked in a breath and turned around. There was a small figure standing in the shadow of the doorway. His heart was pounding in his chest.

"Then step out of the dark and tell me who you are and what you want here."

He held his breath as he prayed, but he didn't know what he was praying for until she came into the light.

She moved forward, and the dim light shone on the small, slender woman with inky-black hair as he remembered. Her face… She was still beautiful, with her perfect olive skin and high cheekbones. It was those eyes, ebony in color and so piercing.

He swallowed back the dryness in his throat. "Lucia?" Was she a dream?

"Yes, it's me, Colt. I came back as soon as I could get here."

He blinked several times, but she was still

there. Suddenly, he felt his anger build, years' worth of anger. "Well, you're too late," he lied. "Too many years late."

The next week had been a blur of activities preparing for the wedding. When the day finally arrived, Garrett helped his son with his tie. They were both in the wedding party.

They'd spent the past two days decorating the lodge for the wedding, and the rehearsal dinner last night had him already exhausted. Today was going to be the end of it. Would it also be the end of his seeing Josie?

"Dad, do you want to get married again?"

Whoa, where did that come from? "I think I'm going to wait awhile for that, son. I have you and Grandpa, and that's enough for me now."

Brody wrinkled his nose. "But Grandpa says that it's really good to have someone to share stuff with. You know, like when you come home from work and she kisses you and makes supper."

"What are you getting at, son?"

The boy shrugged. "I was just thinking maybe it would be nice to have someone to live with us. Someone who gives hugs and kisses at bedtime. I mean, I know I'm almost too big for that, but having a mom again might be nice."

"But your mother..."

"I miss her, and Grandpa says I always will, but he says there's always more room in our hearts to love people. So can we love Josie?"

Boy, could he. He knelt down in front of his son. "If it were that easy, son, I would have figured out a way by now. Josie lives in California."

"Can't she live here?"

"She does weddings and other special parties. She needs a place like this lodge, but bigger."

Brody's green eyes searched Garrett's face. "Well, that's easy. Can't you build her a really big place for all her parties closer to our house?"

CHAPTER THIRTEEN

THE WINTER WONDERLAND scene was perfect for a December wedding.

At seven o'clock the music cued the wedding party to begin the procession down the River's Edge Lodge's staircase. Fresh garlands intertwined with white ribbon had been strung along the banister. Downstairs in front of the picture window were four pine trees decorated with twinkling lights and at the white arch stood pots of bright red poinsettias.

Josie glanced at Ana, dressed in her beautiful antique-white satin gown. The long veil was the perfect touch to highlight the bride's dark hair, pulled away from her pretty face.

Tori and Josie were dressed in dark green ankle-length dresses. Bridesmaid Tori started her descent down the staircase. The only one missing was their youngest sister, Marissa, who couldn't make it that day.

Josie handed Ana a bouquet of blush-colored

roses, then blew a kiss before she made her way down. Immediately, she looked toward the front of the main area where the groom and the best man stood at attention. She smiled at the small group of friends seated on either side of the aisle, but she couldn't take her eyes off Garrett. He looked so handsome in his tux. His dark hair had been cut and styled. Their gazes locked, and she felt a warm tingle all the way to her open-toed heels.

Just make it through today and tomorrow, she thought, knowing she already had her flight booked to leave in two days. And then she could put this all behind her.

Josie arrived at her spot at the end of the aisle. She broke her eye contact with Garrett and smiled at Brody, standing beside his father, then went to her place next to Tori. She stole another glance at Garrett and found him staring at her. The pull was so strong she had to fight to look away. Leaving was getting harder and harder.

The music changed, and Ana appeared at the top of the staircase and walked down alone, then Dad met the bride at the bottom.

Colt Slater drew his eldest daughter into his arms and held her close. Seconds ticked off as the big man blinked away tears and he whispered something to Ana. Finally, he kissed her cheek then offered his arm to her, and together they made their way up the aisle toward her soon-to-be husband.

Once they began to exchange vows, Josie's gaze kept wandering back to Garrett. He was watching her, too. She looked away but felt the heat of his gaze.

Finally, the ceremony was over, and the bride and groom came down the aisle arm in arm. The wedding party was next. Garrett offered Josie his arm and they walked out.

Before he released her, he said, "It was a nice ceremony. You look beautiful, Josie."

"Thank you, but you should be telling the bride that." She loved hearing the words, but it didn't change anything. She was in love with a man she couldn't be with.

Brody rushed up to them. "You look so pretty, Josie. Doesn't she, Dad?"

He winked at her. "Yes, son, she does."

Josie smiled. "Okay, you two flirts, I need to supervise the reception. So I'm off." She headed toward the banquet room past the fireplace. Round tables had been set up, decorated with white linen and multicolored floral centerpieces. At the head of the room was the long bridal party table. She'd be seated with Garrett. She had to blink away the tears. For the last time.

* * *

An hour later, the reception was in full swing. Garrett watched as Vance took Ana in his arms and began to move around the small dance floor. Envy tore at him. His friend went after what he wanted, and he'd found the woman of his dreams.

He watched as Vance kissed Ana, then released her as Colt made his way out to the floor. "Father and daughter dance," the DJ announced. Colt took his oldest daughter in his arms and began to move to the song. It was touching to see how far the man had come to repair the relationship with his daughters.

Then the DJ called for the wedding party to join them. Garrett didn't hesitate and escorted Josie onto the floor. He closed his eyes and drew her against him and prayed he'd be able to find the words to keep her with him. He swayed to the soft ballad, then placed a soft kiss against her forehead.

He danced her off to a corner. "Josie…I need to talk to you."

She shook her head. "I can't, Garrett."

He held her close. "Can't you give me five minutes so I can tell you how I feel?"

"Please, Garrett. We've gone over this so many times."

"Then hear me out once more."

Just then the DJ came up to them. "It's time for the maid of honor and best man's toasts."

Josie took off, but Garrett was stopped by his son. "Dad, did you ask her yet?"

His son looked hopeful. "Look, Brody, I don't think this is going to work. Josie is set on going back to L.A."

"You can't let her. Tell her we love her. A lot. And we want to her stay." The boy squeezed his hand. "Don't be afraid, Dad, 'cause she loves us, too. I know she does."

Garrett nodded and watched as Josie took the microphone and began with a childhood story and then talked about how Vance came to the ranch. Josie also spoke about how much she loved her sister and how lucky Vance was to have her in his life.

After the applause, it was Garrett's turn, and he walked to the front of the room. He looked at Vance and Ana and smiled.

"I can't be any happier for the two of you. Of course, there were times, Ana, that this man was going half-crazy because you wouldn't give him the time of day." Everyone laughed. "I told him to be patient because you were worth it." Garrett sighed. "I hope you two know how lucky you are to find each other."

He turned and looked at Josie. "I know because it's hard to find that special person to love." His gaze met hers, and he was determined to make her hear this. "If you do find her, tell her how much you love her. Tell her how your life is so empty without her in it. Because you might not get another chance." He realized the guests were silent.

He raised his glass as Josie left the room. "To Vance and Ana, may your life together be a long and happy one." He took a drink of champagne, and then hugged the bride, then Vance.

"Go after her, Garrett," his friend said. "Don't let her get away this time."

Josie rushed upstairs into the bedroom they'd used as a dressing room. She paced in front of the window. She couldn't keep doing this. Garrett wanted her. Okay, she wanted him, too, but that didn't mean it would happen.

There was a knock on the door, and Colt peered inside. "If you'd rather be alone, I'll leave."

She fought tears and motioned for him to enter. Without a word she walked into his open arms and let the tears fall.

After a few minutes, he pulled back. "I hate seeing you hurting."

"Some things can't be helped."

"Do you love Garrett?"

"Yes, Dad, I love him. I don't think I ever

stopped loving him, but when he found someone else and had a child... It hurt me."

Colt looked serious. "I'm new at this giving advice stuff, and you might not like what I have to say, but here goes. If my memory is correct, about ten years ago you sent Garrett away. And as for finding someone else, I believe that was months later, after Garrett made several attempts to talk to you." Her father's eyes grew tender. "And the man did the right thing and married the mother of his child. Now he's raising his son alone. Brody is a great kid." Colt tipped her chin up. "I take blame in this, too. I made you girls afraid to trust a man to be there because I was never there for you. I'm so sorry, Josie."

She nodded and wiped her tears.

"Just don't let what I did cloud your judgment toward Garrett. He's a good man and he loves you. You know those second chances are pretty sweet. At least give him that chance to tell you what he wants."

She wrapped her arms around this man. It felt so good. "I love you, Dad."

"I love you, too, Josie," he said in a gruff voice. "Now, go find your guy and put him out of his misery."

Could there be a chance for them? She had to find Garrett. Smiling, she opened the door and there stood Brody.

"Josie, please don't leave. Dad and I want you to stay here with us. He can build you a big building and you can do weddings and parties so you don't have to go back to California."

She pulled the boy into a hug, overwhelmed by a rush of feelings. "Oh, Brody, it's going to be okay. I just need to talk to your father."

Her wish came true, and Garrett appeared in the doorway. "I'm right here."

Her heart stopped then began to race. "Garrett…"

Colt slipped out behind her and took Brody's hand. "How about we let Josie and your dad work things out?" The two walked away, and Josie's fear almost had her running after them.

Garrett wasn't sure he could handle another rejection from her, but at least he wasn't going to do it in public. He guided Josie back into the room and closed the door. "I'm going to give it one more shot, then if you don't like what I have to say, I promise I won't bother you again." He prayed he could find the right words. "Josie, from the second I saw you in high school, you had me. We were both young back then, too young to know what we wanted. No, that's not true. I wanted you. I've always wanted you."

Her eyes were big and so blue. He had to glance away so he could concentrate.

"Ten years ago, when I took that job, I'd

planned to make enough money that summer to buy you an engagement ring. I'd hoped we could be married and I'd take you back to college with me. I couldn't stand being without you."

A tear slid down her face, and he brushed it away. "I'm sorry." She raised a trembling hand to her mouth.

"When you refused to talk to me I nearly quit work and school to come home, but I needed the job for college credit. Natalie Kirkwood was my boss's daughter, so she was around a lot. The first time I went out with her it was to try and forget you." He glanced away again. "I was hurting so much…it just happened between us. But I'll never regret having Brody. My son is the best of me, and I love him."

"He's a wonderful boy," she whispered.

"I'll always care about Natalie because she's Brody's mom. But our marriage was doomed from the start because I still had feelings for you. I want another chance for us."

She blinked back more tears. "Maybe I should be asking for a second chance. I was the one who pushed you away." She shrugged. "I was afraid, Garrett. I knew you wanted to get married, and I panicked."

"Why didn't you tell me?"

Again she shrugged. "I thought you'd leave

me." She gave a tiny laugh. "You left me anyway."

He brushed away the moisture from her cheek. "Like I said, you always had me, Josie." He felt the trembling, but didn't know if it was her or him. "How about we forgive ourselves for the past and start a clean slate?" He took her in his arms. "I love you, Josie Slater. I always have and always will."

"Oh, Garrett, I love you, too."

"I love hearing you say those words again." He dipped his head and covered her mouth in a soft kiss, making him only want more. He took several nibbles, then had to stop. There was so much that needed to be settled between them.

He drew back. "Now we have to find a way to be together. And I don't want a long-distance relationship."

She raised an eyebrow. "Brody said something about you wanting to build a place for my weddings and parties."

He couldn't help but smile. "So my son's been playing my pitchman. I had to talk to him about the future, Josie. We are a package deal."

Josie realized that she wanted Brody in her life as much as his father. "You are so lucky to have that boy. I'm already crazy about him."

Garrett hesitated, then finally said, "I'm asking a lot of you, Josie, to take on an eight-year-old child, my father and me. And if it was just us two, I'd follow you back to L.A. But I can't leave. So I'm offering to help you build a business here. I know Royerton might not be able to handle enough work for an event planner. Maybe Butte, or Bozeman, and I'll build you another lodge, a wedding chapel, a retreat. You name whatever you want, and I'll do what I can to get it for you."

She couldn't believe he was doing all this for her. "You. I want you...and Brody and Nolan in my life."

"God, I love you." He picked her up and swung her around, then finally put her down.

She raised a hand. "I'll still need to travel back and forth to L.A. until I finish out the contracts I've already signed. But I'm ready now to be with the man I love."

"That's music to my ears," he told her, then covered her mouth with his. He nudged her lips with his tongue, and she opened eagerly to welcome him. He finally broke off the kiss. "You are one big distraction."

She was too dazed to react to what happened next. He drew back and lowered to one knee.

"I hadn't planned to do this here, but I'm not about to let you get away again. Josie Slater, I love you with all my heart. Would you do me the honor of being my wife and the mother to my son and all the other children we may have together?"

Tears flowed again. "Oh, Garrett. Yes! Yes, I'll marry you."

He kissed her tenderly, and she melted into his arms, nearly forgetting where they were. That's when she heard the commotion downstairs.

"Oh, gosh, the wedding. We've got to get back."

Josie opened the door and, almost giddy, they rushed along the open railing to the top of the staircase. Looking down, she found the wedding party and guests in front of the picture window. Ana was standing alone with a line of ladies about twenty feet away. "Oh, she's going to toss the bouquet," Josie said.

Ana looked up and spotted them. "Josie you're just in time. Come on down, I'm going to throw my bouquet."

Josie looked at Garrett.

He grinned at her, then he addressed the crowd. "Josie Slater isn't going to be single for very much longer. She's just agreed to marry me."

The crowd cheered as Ana walked to the staircase. "Then this is rightfully yours." Her sister tossed the bouquet toward the balcony. Josie leaned forward and snatched it out of the air.

She blushed as everyone applauded and Garrett pulled her into his arms. "It's too late to back out now."

"No way. I have everything I've always wanted."

She touched her lips to his. She knew she didn't have to give up anything, because this man was what she'd always wanted and so much more.

EPILOGUE

THREE DAYS AFTER Ana and Vance's wedding, Colt was alone for the first time since his stroke. The newlyweds were off on their honeymoon, and Josie and Garrett had flown to L.A. to deal with her business and the town house cleanup. Tori had gone off to visit an old school friend in town, and it was Kathleen's day off.

It was all set. Colt was free to go to his meeting without any questions. Only his friend and lawyer, Wade, knew what had been going on. He had to confide in someone.

"Are you sure you want to do this?" Wade asked as he glanced away from the road leading to Dillon.

"Hell, no, I'm not sure of anything, except I have to see her." He looked at his friend. "I need to hear her reason for why she left."

"What about the girls?" Wade asked.

He felt a little traitorous for not telling his daughters. "I'm not going to tell 'em, yet. Not until Lucia convinces me she doesn't want to claim something that isn't hers."

"I think maybe you should wait until the P.I. has finished checking things out."

Colt sighed. That would be the wise thing, but when it came to Lucia Delgado, he hadn't always acted wisely. "All I'm doing is listening to what she has to say."

Wade stayed silent as they pulled into the chain hotel parking lot. Colt and Wade got out of the car and walked through the double doors. He looked into the restaurant/lounge to see it was nearly empty except for a woman seated at a corner booth.

Colt squared his shoulders as his stomach took a tumble. She looked across the room, then stood up. His breath caught. She was dressed in a leather jacket and a black turtleneck sweater with a bright scarf around her slender neck. Even though she was wearing jeans, there was no way this woman wouldn't turn heads.

"Damn…" Wade breathed from behind him. "It's like time has stood still. I'll be at the bar if you need me."

Colt started across the room, careful his steps were sure and true. The last thing he wanted was to fall on his face. He had some pride. He made his way through the empty tables until he stood in front of his ex-wife.

"Lucia." Even at the age of fifty-two, he was slammed in his gut by her beauty.

"Hello, Colt."

Even though he'd expected her, he couldn't believe she was really here. "We should get this over with." He motioned for her to sit, then he slid into the booth across from her.

Although it was dim in the room, he stared into those incredible dark eyes. "It's been a long time, Lucia."

Not counting the night she'd come into his room. Then she'd called him yesterday and asked to meet with him.

"Yes, it has." Her voice was soft and throaty.

He felt as shaky as a teenager. "Okay, I agreed to talk to you, so we should get started." The waitress appeared and he ordered some coffee. He wanted something stronger, but knew that wasn't wise. He needed a clear head.

The waitress came back with two coffee cups and a cream pitcher. Lucia looked surprised when he pushed the creamer toward her.

"You remember how I like my coffee." The words came out in a soft voice.

"I remember a lot of things. The sound of your voice as you read stories to our babies. How you cuddled them in your arms, how you loved them."

He drew a breath and worked hard to release

it. "I also remember the way it felt to make love to you, to hear your gasps of pleasure." He watched her eyes widen, her face flush. "I also remember you saying you loved me, that you loved the girls. Then the next day you disappeared from our lives."

She stayed silent for a long time, and then said, "I had no choice, Colton."

"There's always a choice, Lucia. You chose to leave your family…your *bambinas,* your *marido.*" *Husband.*

She shook her head. "You have to believe me, *mi amor.*"

"No! You can't call me your love. The woman I married, the woman I loved would never leave me. I don't know who you are."

Lucia stiffened and pulled back. So she still had a temper. "I never wanted to leave my family, *mi corazon.*" *My heart.* There was a fierce look in her ebony eyes, and his body betrayed him as he reacted to her.

"And you were my heart, too, Lucia. I gave you everything, but you left anyway."

"You don't understand," she insisted. "I gave up my *familia* to keep you from harm."

He frowned. "You're saying that someone wanted to harm us?"

He saw her hands shake as she nodded.

"Who was this person?"

"Vicente Santoya... My husband."

Her declaration was like a knife to his heart. Of course, she'd been with other men. Was Santoya the reason she'd left him?

"I don't want to hear about your lovers." He was unable to keep the anger out of his voice. "I've made a life without you. So you can just go back to him." Hell, he didn't need this. He'd learned to live without her before—he could do it again. He started to get out of the booth. Then she placed her hand on his and stopped him.

"*Por favor,* Colt! I can't go back there. It took me too long to get out. Vicente is dead. So I've broken most of my ties there. So I can safely come back...to you."

He didn't want to hear about her marriage. "What about your father?" Cesar Delgado never wanted his only child to marry an American, especially a broken-down, ex-rodeo cowboy. How did he feel about her return to Montana?

Lucia straightened and looked him in the eye. "My parents are gone. My ties and loyalty are only to this country. So please, I ask that you hear what I have to say before you send me away."

He wasn't going to be fooled again. Lucia had made a life for herself without him. "I don't see how anything that you have to say will change my mind."

She looked nervous, almost panicky. "What if it concerns your sons?"

He shook his head. "I don't have sons."

Lucia nodded. "Yes, you do. I was pregnant with twin boys when I left you."

Five days later, a happy Garrett and Josie arrived back in Montana. The only reason she'd wanted to stay in L.A. a little longer was because Josie had liked having her man all to herself. Still, she knew they needed to get back. She had a wedding to plan.

She was also able to start her life in Montana because she had a great assistant. That was why she'd offered Megan Buckner a partnership in the business. Megan had eagerly accepted the deal. So Josie would be able to wean herself from her L.A. projects and not cancel a single event.

Garrett reached across the seat and took her hand as he drove down the road. "Would you mind if we made a quick stop in town first?"

"Not a problem, but I want to be at the house so we can meet Brody's bus."

"I thought we could pick him up at school after I show you something."

She smiled. "I like that idea better." She was so anxious to see the child. She couldn't believe how easily she'd fallen in love with the eight-year-old boy. Of course all the Temple men were very appealing.

At the end of Main Street, Garrett turned into the driveway of a three-story Victorian house. The huge structure showed years of neglect with faded and peeling paint, and the wraparound porch needed a railing at the very least.

"Isn't this Mrs. Anderson's house?"

Garrett put the truck into Park and shut off the engine. "Yes, but she died last year and her daughter inherited it. She wants to sell the place." He rubbed his hand along the back of his neck. "I thought with a little rehab and TLC it would make a great office for Slater Style and maybe even a place to hold some small events. The large backyard could be landscaped for weddings."

Josie was suddenly excited. "I want to go see it." She jumped out of the car and rushed to the door. She tried the knob but it was locked.

"Hold on." Garrett came after her, put a key into the lock and got it open. "Now, don't get too excited," he warned. "It needs some work."

She kissed him. "I'm going to love it, but not as much as I love you for doing this," she said as she walked inside.

The entry was huge, with a crystal chandelier hanging from the high ceiling. The staircase was a work of art, with a hand-carved banister that ran up to the second floor, and stained-glass windows above the landing.

There were raised-panel pocket doors that could close off the three large rooms downstairs. The hardwood floors needed refinishing, but there would soon be a contractor in the family.

She was a little giddy as she walked down the hall to a kitchen that was in really bad condition.

Garrett came up behind her. "This needs a gut job, honey. But we can make it look like the era of the home. Anything you want."

"You're spoiling me."

"Get used to it." He turned her around and lowered his mouth to hers for a kiss that was slow and easy. The result had her breathless.

"I plan to make sure you're happy working here."

"I have you and Brody in my life, and that makes everything just about perfect."

She brushed another kiss on his tempting mouth, then went to check every nook and cranny of the area, which included a large pantry and sunroom off the kitchen. Then she opened the back door into a yard that seemed to go on forever. A high fence circled the property and there was a gazebo toward the back.

"Oh, Garrett, it's lovely."

Garrett came up behind her and wrapped his arms around her to ward off the winter cold.

"I'm glad you like it. You've had to make all the sacrifices, Josie. So I wanted you to have this house." He loved her so much. "Your career is important."

She smiled at him, and his heart raced. "Being with you and Brody doesn't feel like a sacrifice to me. And I get to be around my family, too. Ana and Dad." She shook her head. "Can you believe I'm calling Colt, Dad?"

"You have to give him credit, Josie. He's trying hard with you girls."

"I know." She shook her head. "Now, if I can convince Tori to stay around for a while." She frowned. "At least until we're sure that Dane is out of her life."

"Richards is working on that. Until then, I promise I'll do everything possible to keep her here and keep her safe."

She smiled. "I love you so much, Garrett Temple. I can't wait to start our life together."

He pulled her into his arms. He wanted that to happen very soon. "About that. I was wondering when that special day is going to take place. I'm not happy about you still living in your dad's house."

They'd both decided because Brody was at an impressionable age, that they wouldn't live together until after the wedding.

"How soon can you get the renovations done here?" she asked.

"That depends on what you want done."

"The downstairs. The floors refinished and some new paint."

"A few weeks, maybe a month with a new kitchen. The crew can start renovations right after Christmas."

She sighed. "Christmas is only ten days away. I've always hated the holiday...." She glanced up at him. "Until now. Now, I get you, Brody and my family."

"I'm gonna make it special for you," he told her. "We'll start some good memories."

Josie held up her hand to inspect the diamond solitaire engagement ring he'd bought her in Los Angeles. "Oh, I do believe you've already made everything very special." She glanced back at the yard. "So how do you feel about having the wedding right here?"

Garrett arched an eyebrow. "Outside?"

"Oh, I'd love that. A garden wedding, but even I don't want to wait that long. How about Valentine's Day in the front parlor?"

"If that's what you want, I'll work day and night to get this place ready." He grinned. "And it will be great advertising for future weddings at Slater Manor."

Josie had trouble holding on to her emotions.

"Slater Manor…" She repeated the name over in her head. "I like that, but how about Temple Manor?"

He shook his head. "No, Josie. You've worked hard to build a name with Slater Style. Slater Manor makes good business sense." He smiled. "I still want you to take my name for everything else."

"I've waited a long time for you, Garrett Temple. So only in business will I use Slater." She swallowed hard. She bravely went on, hoping he wanted the same thing. "And while you're doing the renovations, could you make a nursery upstairs?"

This time she watched him swallow hard. "A nursery? A baby nursery?"

She nodded. "So I can work and keep our babies with me."

"I would love that. But not as much as making a child with you," he whispered as he placed kisses along her jaw to her ear, finally reaching her mouth. The kiss was hungry, letting her know he desired her. When he released her, she could see he'd been as affected as she was.

"God, we're so lucky, Josie. We got a second chance." He cupped her face. "There's never been anyone I've loved as much as you. There's no one else I want to spend the rest of my life with."

She smiled. "Then it's a good thing you don't have to, because I'm not leaving you ever again."

"And this time, I'd just follow you, because you are my heart." He kissed her again, holding her close.

Josie held on, too. She'd stopped running away. She'd found everything right here. She would never feel alone again.

* * * * *

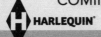
#4403 SECOND CHANCE WITH HER SOLDIER
Barbara Hannay

When Corporal Joe Madden returns to his estranged wife, Ellie, he wants her signature on the divorce papers. But stranded together in bad weather, could a Christmas truce bring the sparkle back into their marriage?

#4404 SNOWED IN WITH THE BILLIONAIRE
Caroline Anderson

Childhood sweethearts Georgia Beckett and Sebastian Corder are each other's refuge in a blizzard. Is it time to give their love a second chance?

#4405 CHRISTMAS AT THE CASTLE
Marion Lennox

When Angus Stuart offers Holly McIntosh the *temporary* position of chef in his castle, she's determined to make it permanent. Can she melt the Earl's brooding heart?

#4406 SNOWFLAKES AND SILVER LININGS
The Gingerbread Girls
Cara Colter

When Casey Caravetta meets Turner, her ex, at a Christmas wedding, it *doesn't* inspire much festive cheer. But maybe a little bit of holiday magic is just what they've been waiting for....

**YOU CAN FIND MORE INFORMATION
ON UPCOMING HARLEQUIN® TITLES,
FREE EXCERPTS AND MORE AT
WWW.HARLEQUIN.COM.**

HRLPCNM1113

SPECIAL EXCERPT FROM

**Celebrate Christmas next month with Cara Colter's
Snowflakes and Silver Linings, the third and final story
in the sparkling Gingerbread Girls trilogy!**

Turner Kennedy had seen her as no one else ever had. But
she had seen him, too, felt she had known things about him.
Now, studying his face as he squinted up toward the porch
ceiling, she put her finger on what was different about him.

During those playful days, Turner Kennedy had seemed
hopeful and filled with confidence. He had told her about
losing his dad under very hard circumstances, but she had
been struck by a certain faith in himself to change all that was
bad about the world.

Now Casey was aware she was looking into the face of a
warrior—calm, strong, watchful. Ready.

And also, deeply weary. There was a hard-edged cynicism
about him that went deeper than cynical. It went to his soul.

Casey knew that just as she had known things about him
all those years ago. It was as if, with him, she arrived at a
different level of knowing with almost terrifying swiftness.

And the other thing she knew?

Turner Kennedy was ready to protect her with his life.

A second passed and then two, but they were long, drawn-
out seconds, as if time had come to an amazing standstill.

This was what chemicals did, she told herself dreamily. He
thought, apparently, they were in mortal danger.

She was bathing in the intoxicating closeness of him.

HREXP1113

Casey could feel the strong beat of his heart through the thin fabric of his shirt. He was radiating a silky, sensual warmth, and she could feel the exact moment that his muscles began to uncoil. She observed the watchfulness drain from his expression, felt the thud of his heart quieting.

Finally, he looked away from the roof and gazed intently down at her.

Now that his mind had sounded some kind of all clear, he, too, seemed to be feeling the pure chemistry of their closeness. His breath caressed her face like the touch of a summer breeze. She could feel her own heart picking up tempo as his began to slow. His mouth dropped closer to hers.

The new her, the one who was going to be impervious to the chemistry of pure attraction, seemed to be sitting passively in the backseat instead of the driver's seat. Because instead of giving Turner a much-deserved shove—fight—or scooting out from under him—flight—she licked her lips, and watched his eyes darken and his lips drop even closer to hers.

Don't miss *Snowflakes and Silver Linings*, available December 2013–the third and final installment from the Gingerbread Girls!

Copyright © 2013 by Collette Caron

HREXP1113

HARLEQUIN® Romance

Second Chance with Her Soldier
by Barbara Hannay

One last chance?

His blue eyes seemed to penetrate all the way to her soul. Her heart began to gallop. She couldn't back down now that she'd begun.

Corporal Joe Madden knows his once perfect marriage is set for the final curtain. It might be three years since Ellie saw her husband, yet his power to make her heart race is just as strong. Could a Christmas peace treaty and a magical few days bring the sparkle back into their marriage?

Look for
SECOND CHANCE WITH HER SOLDIER
by Barbara Hannay, coming next month
from Harlequin Romance!

Available wherever books and ebooks are sold.

www.Harlequin.com

HR74268